# Heart the Lover

**Also by Lily King**

*Five Tuesdays in Winter*
*Writers & Lovers*
*Euphoria*
*Father of the Rain*
*The English Teacher*
*The Pleasing Hour*

# Heart the Lover

A NOVEL

## LILY KING

Grove Press
*New York*

Copyright © 2025 by Lily King

All rights reserved. No part of this book may be reproduced in any form or by any electronic or mechanical means, including information storage and retrieval systems, without permission in writing from the publisher, except by a reviewer, who may quote brief passages in a review. Scanning, uploading, and electronic distribution of this book or the facilitation of such without the permission of the publisher is prohibited. Please purchase only authorized electronic editions, and do not participate in or encourage electronic piracy of copyrighted materials. Your support of the author's rights is appreciated. Any member of educational institutions wishing to photocopy part or all of the work for classroom use, or anthology, should send inquiries to Grove Atlantic, 154 West 14th Street, New York, NY 10011 or permissions@groveatlantic.com.

Author's note: The fictional story "The Last Fall" is inspired by David Updike's beautiful short story "Bachelor of Arts." Many thanks to Michael Goldfinger for medical advice, and to everyone in my life for their love and kindness.

Any use of this publication to train generative artificial intelligence ("AI") technologies is expressly prohibited. The author and publisher reserve all rights to license uses of this work for generative AI training and development of machine learning language models.

FIRST EDITION

By Céline, translated by Ralph Manheim, from *Journey to the End of the Night*, copyright © 1934, 1952 by Louis-Ferdinand Céline, Translation copyright © 1983 Ralph Manheim. Reprinted by permission of New Directions Publishing Corp. and Alma Classics.

*Printed in the United States of America*

This book was typeset in 11.5-pt. Bembo by Alpha Design & Composition of Pittsfield, NH.

First Grove Atlantic hardcover edition: October 2025

Library of Congress Cataloging-in-Publication data is available for this title.

ISBN 978-0-8021-6517-6
eISBN 978-0-8021-6518-3

Grove Press
an imprint of Grove Atlantic
154 West 14th Street
New York, NY 10011

Distributed by Publishers Group West

groveatlantic.com

25 26 27 28   10 9 8 7 6 5 4 3 2 1

For Tyler, Calla, and Eloise,
loves of my heart

I

You knew I'd write a book about you someday. You said once that I'd dredged up the whole hit parade minus you.

I'll never know how you'd tell it.

For me it begins here. Like this.

The professor is holding up two neon-orange pieces of paper.

'Despite its vulgar packaging,' he says, waving a page in each hand like a flagman at Daytona, 'I feel compelled to read this one aloud.'

The assignment had been to write a contemporary version of Bacon's essay 'History of Life and Death.' I'd waited till the last minute to write it. The only paper we had in the house was this thick stuff left over from our Halloween party. And it wasn't easy, feeding that cardstock into my typewriter.

The professor doesn't read it as much as perform it. He gives it far more life and humor than I imagined it had.

There are two smart guys in the class. They sit up front together and I see only the backs of their heads, one with coppery brown hair and the other with a thick black ponytail. The professor runs things by them so often I assume they're his grad school TAs. When my essay gets passed back to me, they both turn to watch where it goes.

After that day, the copper-haired one begins migrating back. Three classes later, he takes a seat beside me.

Soon he is walking me across campus to Modern Furniture, the only art history class that wasn't full by the time I signed up. Our seventeenth-century lit class has only about thirty people, but Modern Furniture is held in an auditorium with cushioned seats set on a steep slope down to the professor at his podium. Behind him is a big screen that flashes pictures of Corbusier's B 306 chaise longue and Bauhaus nesting tables. I catch up on a lot of sleep in that class.

Sam has short halting steps and speaks in fits and starts too, little articulate bursts then a good bit of silence. We talk exclusively about the class.

'He's not focusing enough on Cromwell,' he says, 'and how resistance to him galvanized the imagination of this whole generation of writers.'

I agree. What else can I do? I am a mere student, and he is a scholar. That much is clear right away. I've never met a scholar who wasn't a professor. And Sam isn't even a grad student. He's a senior, like me.

Later I go to the library and read about who Cromwell was, and the next time we walk to Modern Furniture I make a very small joke about the Rump Parliament. Sam's laugh is soundless, more like panting.

He asks me if I've seen *The Deer Hunter* and I say yes and I figure he's going to make a comparison somehow with Venitore, the hunter, in *The Compleat Angler*. Instead he asks me if I want to see it again, with him. It's playing on campus Friday night.

We meet at the Student Union. He's already bought my ticket. They've set up rows of metal chairs and a screen on a stand. We sit and wait for the lights to go out. My roommate, Carson, passes us with her boyfriend, Bud, a Green Beret who drives up from Fort Bragg every chance he gets. They're arguing as they sidestep to empty seats three rows ahead of us and then, once settled, start groping each other.

The movie starts. It is long and brutal. I have to look down into my lap for half of it. Sam sits like a stranger beside me. Finally they sing 'God Bless America' at the dinner table after Christopher Walken's funeral, the frame freezes, and it is over. Sam gets up as soon as the credits roll, and I follow him out of the Student Union.

We head down a campus path that isn't in the direction of my room on Pye Street or toward town, where I thought we might get a drink. He points out his dorm from freshman year and I point out mine the next quad over. The movie has made these buildings, these quads, these years of our lives seem unbearably naïve. I want to say something about it, but that feels naïve, too. Instead I start to say that I have to get up early and he asks if I'd like to get a beer.

We walk toward the bars, but he veers onto a side street then through the gate of a white fence and up a stepping-stone path to a front door lit by an overhead light.

'Where are we?'

'My house.'

I can tell he wanted to show it to me, knew it would be a draw.

It is.

He turns the knob—the house is unlocked—and holds the door open for me. I step into a small vestibule with steep stairs off to the left. To the right is a little table with a lamp and a pad of paper with a pen on top. Through an open door is a living room painted navy blue with a striped couch and a wall of books.

I remark on the number of books.

'That's just the overspill,' he says. I follow him through the living room into a large study out of an old movie—four walls of floor-to-ceiling books, a big, thick-legged desk, and a leather chair before the fireplace.

'Is this where you smoke your pipe in the evening?'

With a small smile he pulls open the top drawer of the table beside the leather chair to reveal four old pipes nestled neatly on a wooden rack.

I laugh and he pants.

'Whose house is this?'

'Dr. Gastrell's. Did you ever have him for Chaucer? Or his seminar on Milton?'

I shake my head. I've heard of Gastrell before. 'Gastric,' people call him. Stay away, I've heard, he's notoriously hard. Can undergrads actually take seminars?

'He's on sabbatical, doing research at Merton.' He sees my lack of recognition. 'At Oxford. He asked us to take care of the place for the year.'

'Us?'

'Yash and me.'

Yash?

There's so much he expects me to know.

Neither of us is sure what to say after that. Sam shuts the drawer with the pipes and I ask where the bathroom is. He points to a sloped door beneath the stairs. I don't really have to go. I just need to be alone for a minute. The toilet bowl is deep and the tiny bit I pee makes a loud sound when it hits the water, so I stop. The mirror above the sink is an oval fixed high on the wall. I can see half my forehead at a time, one eye or the other, if I stand on tiptoe.

The hallway is empty, the door out to the street a few steps away. In ten minutes I could be back in my room on Pye Street. But Carson and Bud will be there going at it in one way or another. A refrigerator opens and I follow the sound.

We sit with our bottles of beer on the striped couch in the navy room. Its cushions are stiff and we are stiff and he isn't a guy who's afraid of the long pause. We pick at our labels and speak sporadically. He asks if I have a lot of work this weekend and I say I have to write a short story.

'Why?'

'For my fiction class.'

He nods slowly, full of some thought he's decided not to share. 'What will you write about?'

I look around the room. 'Tonight, probably.'

He looks alarmed. Then he pants. 'Good one.'

The front door opens and slams against the wall.

'Fucking fucking hell,' says a voice from the hallway. The door shudders shut. 'I'm locking it in case she followed me.' A whoop-laugh. 'You here? How was the daisy?' He swings into the room, the other guy from our class. Yash. 'Oh my. If she isn't right here before us.'

His hair is out of its ponytail, thick and black, just past his shoulders. He is trying hard to stop laughing.

'The *daisy*?' I say.

'Date, daisy,' he says. 'We call all our dates daisies. And my daisy tonight was a doozy.' He smiles wide and comes closer. I glance at Sam, worried that he's going to kick him out, but he's got a little grin on his face I haven't seen yet. He's as relieved as I am that there are three of us now.

'What happened?' he says.

'Well, I go and pick her up at Kappa,' Yash says, standing in front of the coffee table facing us. Sam and I lean back at the same time, as if we've turned on a TV.

'You have to sign in and give blood and take a vow of chastity and then you have to wait in a fucking parlor with *doilies* on all the tables for twenty minutes with all the other pathetic dudes. God, that guy Ian was there—the one who quoted Victor Hugo's last words.'

Sam chuckles. 'I see black light.'

'I saw black light at Kappa for sure. It's creepy in that room, and sort of smelly too, like if I get a whiff of my mother's fingers, all the stuff she's poked her fingers in during the day.' He looks at me and jabs a finger in the air a few times. 'My mother is a real poker,' he says. 'Finally we hear steps on the stairs and these girls all come down together and they look kind of alike and now none of us remember anymore who we're taking out because we've been stuck in that playpen all night. However, someone identifies me from the lineup and we get the hell out of there. I take her to Pip's, we talk about her father, who has some rare ghastly disease, and her brother, who sounds like an a-hole, and I order something that should have been called maroon glop over dirty sponge and bring her back to Kappa. She wants to *show* me something back in the playpen, which is now empty and very dimly lit, and I have to look at some god-awful Confederate musket on the wall, which she reveals belonged to her *grandfather*, and I head fast for the door, but her legs are suddenly ten feet long and she gets there first and presses me up against some coat hooks and unhinges her jaw like a snake. It was terrifying. I make a break and manage to get the screen door between us'—he holds up the imaginary door like a shield—'and say goodnight politely and run.'

Sam is laughing so hard he makes sound.

Yash snorts and apologizes and wipes his eyes. He straightens up and wiggles his fingers at us. 'I hope this is going a little better.'

'It's a little awkward,' I say, and they both laugh.

'It'll get better. Sam is an acquired taste,' he says. 'Bonne nuit.' And he clomps up the stairs.

Sam gets up and shuts both doors to the living room. When he sits back down on the couch, he's closer.

'The daisy? Please tell me not as in Daisy Buchanan.'

'In a good way,' he says, and kisses me.

On Monday Sam walks me to Modern Furniture, and when I get out fifty minutes later he's waiting.

'Want to come over for lunch?'

We eat turkey sandwiches and make out on the couch again. He doesn't rush things. We kiss and kiss until I have to go to Logic.

I walk across campus a little lightheaded. I keep bursting out laughing, thinking about making out on Doc Gastric's couch on a Monday in broad daylight. All the awkwardness dissolved when we were kissing. He said little things and I said little things and we made each other laugh on that striped couch.

Could he tell how little experience I'd had? Only one boyfriend so far, Jay, the year before. We met in the fall and I brought him home for spring break and fell out of love with him in my mother's kitchen. I told him on the plane back to school, which is a terrible place to break up. He cried and thrashed around but wouldn't get up and go to the bathroom to pull himself together. The conversation started quietly enough, with him saying what he often said to me, which was that I bottled up my feelings until they came out like a fire hose, that if I didn't withhold so much we could reach each other better. But as he slowly realized that he wasn't going to be able to talk me out of my decision, his recriminations got louder. He'd paid for our *flights*. He could have gone to *Key West* with his friends instead of a *shitty* town in *Massachusetts*. His mother thought I was *lesbian*. 'I taught you everything I know about sex!' he hollered all the way down the aisle into the cockpit, which had no door back then. It was true. He had. I'd been a virgin and he'd been a fun and loving guide. I'd had nothing to compare him or our sex to at the time, but now I know that he was particularly uninhibited and passed along that attitude to me. He did not like that now I was going to pass it along to someone else. He got very hung up on that fact. It was the longest flight of my life, and I was grateful when the wheels hit the runway and my freedom was near. After Jay, I made out with the bartender at the restaurant I worked at, with a guy at the senior pig roast at the start of the semester, and most recently with a friend of Carson's who had also dressed up as Cyndi Lauper for our Halloween party.

Sam invites me for dinner on Friday. I imagine having the house to ourselves, Dr. Gastrell's candlesticks lit in the dining room. At the door, I hand him a bottle of wine.

Sam looks at the label and puts his arm out for me to go into the living room.

'We're pairing a 1987 Riesling with the pepperoni this evening,' he says behind me to Yash and a guy I don't know on the couch. This guy has a mat of ginger curls six inches thick on top of his head. He has short legs and big sneakers splayed on top of Dr. Gastrell's polished coffee table. Beside the sneakers are four boxes of pizza. Yash goes to fetch some wineglasses.

Ginger guy points at me. 'Freshman year. Stranger mixer. You went with Dale Greensmith.'

'This is Ivan,' Sam says.

Ivan shuts his eyes. 'Red dress. Black buttons.'

'Well you're freaky.'

'I'm right, aren't I?'

'About the dress. The date I don't remember.'

They laugh like I'm lying, like you could never remember a dress better than a guy.

'In Riesling veritas,' Yash says, pouring the wine into small, impossibly thin glasses the shape of bluebells. 'We'll get to the truth about old Dale Greensmith before the end of the night.'

Sam and I sit in the armchairs across from Yash and Ivan. The wine is sweet and foul, but I love holding the fragile little glass in my fingers.

Ivan is another English major I've never met before. 'Tell me everything, bar-none everything, that comes to mind when you think about James Joyce,' he says.

Fortunately my high school English teacher was a little obsessed with Joyce. 'Stream of consciousness, onomatopoeia, epiphany, yes I will yes I said Yes, and falling softly, softly falling on the living and the dead.'

Ivan presses the heels of his hands into his eyeballs and rocks his head back and forth. '"Falling faintly through the universe and faintly falling, like the descent of their last end, upon all the living and the dead." I'm so fucked,' he whines.

'He's writing his thesis on *Finnegan's Wake*,' Sam says.

Ivan parts his hands to look at me with a last shred of hope. But I've never heard of it.

'Are you writing a thesis?' I ask Sam.

'You have to, in the honors program.'

'Oh, right.' The *honors* program. I feel like I go to a different college, and they know it.

'Who have you taken?' Ivan asks.

It was that kind of thing. They don't ask what classes but which professors.

I strain a little to think of some names. 'Brody, Iyengar, Doukas.' They were the only ones that came to mind.

No recognition.

'They teach creative writing.'

'Those poor fucks,' Ivan says. Sam signals something to him. 'I just mean, what could be worse than reading crappy stories all semester?'

'They're not crappy anymore. I'm in advanced.' You had to take 101, 201, and 301 to get into advanced.

'Oh, *advanced*.' Ivan laughs.

'I took a creative writing class freshman year,' Yash says.

'No you didn't,' Sam says.

'I did. With Iyengar.' He looks at me. 'She *hated* my story.'

'That is not true,' Sam says.

'*Hated* it.'

'There were little checkmarks and a nice comment.'

'Two checkmarks in fifteen pages, and the comment was patronizing.'

'It wasn't.'

'This shows future promise.' He grimaces.

'It was probably the first paper you'd ever gotten back without the word "genius" or "*incandescent*,"' Sam says, 'at the bottom.'

'It's not that. It isn't. But "future promise"? Like someday far from now I may show the faintest flicker of talent?'

'So you never took another one?' I ask.

'No.'

'He didn't even take that one,' Sam says. 'He dropped it after three weeks.'

'None of the writers I admire ever took a class in creative writing,' Yash says. 'I think I'll be okay.'

Ivan passes me a slice of pizza on a delicate white plate with a gold rim and a cluster of rosebuds in the center. 'Apart from the night of the red dress, why have we never seen you before?' he asks me. 'Where have you been hiding?'

I wasn't in a sorority and I didn't go to frat parties and I worked at a restaurant three nights a week. 'I don't know. I was on the golf team for my first year, so I traveled a lot.' This is stretching the truth a bit.

'You were on the fucking golf team?' he says. Our university has a very good golf team—ACC Champions eleven years straight.

'Freshman year. Then I quit.' I quit the first week.

'Damn. You were a recruit.'

'Everyone's a recruit.' Did he think it was 1920? No one walked on anymore.

'She's not Daisy Buchanan, she's Jordan Baker,' Yash says, then bends an ear toward me. 'Does your voice sound like money?'

'No. It sounds like someone who gave up her golf scholarship.'

I can tell they all like me better once they've changed my name to Jordan. They use it a lot.

Yash carries the empty pizza boxes into the kitchen and comes back with cards. 'Surely Jordan knows how to play hearts.'

I don't, but I love card games and am a quick learner and shoot the moon in the second hand.

'Jordan. Sly J. Watch out there, Sammy.'

Sam glances quickly at me, that little smile above his fan of cards.

'Well,' says Sam after we play six hands, gathering up all the cards and not dealing them out again.

'Time to show her your etchings?' Ivan says. 'There are actual etchings in his room. God's truth.'

'Have a look?' Sam is blushing and also asking me with his eyes.

Yash is loading the dishwasher in the kitchen.

I nod.

In the hallway he takes my hand and I follow him up the tight steep staircase. There's a turn at the top then two more steps. He reaches for a switch on the wall. An old sconce comes on after a delay, dimly. He leads me into the front bedroom. He doesn't turn on the overhead and we don't look at any etchings. He pulls me onto Dr. Gastrell's tall double bed.

We kiss and wrap our legs around each other and he says he's been wanting to get me up here all night. We press hard against each other and I feel like I might come before I get my jeans off. We laugh because my fingers don't seem to be working but I get them unzipped and he reaches for me as soon as I kick them off and he makes a sort of low growl when he feels how wet I am. I feel him, too, straining against the zipper of his jeans. I reach for his belt and he says something that sounds like no. I can feel his pulse through the fabric, the shape of his tip. It takes all my strength to remain still. He kisses me and starts to finger me and doesn't explain why I can't touch him.

I sit up and pull my pants back on. The desire is still careening around inside me, irritatingly, like being drunk when you need to be sober.

'Please don't take it the wrong way,' he says.

I can hear Yash and Ivan arguing downstairs, a few thuds, then Yash laughing. I feel mortified, like the two of them already know what has happened. Ivan sent us up here. He knew how it would play out. I have a paranoid streak and I need to get out of here.

I put on my shoes, adjust my bra, and open the door.

'Jordan.' Sam can move very quickly. He touches my arm, my hip. Lifts my shirt and strokes it with his thumb. 'Please stay. Please, please, please. I can explain.' His lips in my hair, his thumb moving over my hipbone. I don't want to go downstairs and see Yash and Ivan on my way out. Eventually I relent.

We get under the sheets. We keep our shirts and underwear on. He spoons me and kisses my neck and my ear, and my body is in a riot. I need to leave. I need to stay. I can feel him hard against me. I never felt anything like this for Jay. He falls asleep way before I do and does not explain.

I wake up early. I need to go in search of a bathroom. I slip off the bed without waking Sam. Once more I put on my jeans and open the door. The sconce is still on and there are two doors at the end of the hallway. Both shut. My guess is that the bathroom will be above the kitchen because of the plumbing, so I open the door on the left slowly, just a crack.

It's not a bathroom. It's Yash in a twin bed under a yellow bedspread. He is surrounded by books. Books in piles along the walls and all around the bed, and a few beside him on the yellow bedspread. He's on his back with a concentrated, serious expression I've never seen before, as if sleep were very hard work. I shut the door and go into the bathroom across the hall.

Sam is awake when I come back. I get in beside him and there's a lot of kissing and pressing together. With Jay I never liked sex in the morning, but sexual frustration in the morning is even worse. I try to distract myself by looking over his shoulder at the spines of the books on his bedside table. *Confessions of Saint Augustine, Paul the Apostle, Mere Christianity.*

Oh.

'I'm hungry,' I say. 'I should get going.'

'I'll make you breakfast.'

We go down to the kitchen.

It's a neglected, old-fashioned kitchen with a chipped ceramic sink and big black and white tiles on the floor. There's a back door with a glass window and a little yard outside with one sad chair perched in the overgrown grass. I sit at the small table against the wall beside the old fridge. Sam makes coffee in one of those percolators with a plastic cylinder at the top that shows the coffee splashing around. He keeps his back to me even while he's waiting for the water to boil.

He fills the cups and asks me if I take milk. I don't take coffee so I say no, and he says good, we don't have any milk, and pants out a laugh. He sits down opposite me at the table and takes long pulls of the coffee with his eyes closed then gets up for a second cup. To me coffee is gross and only parents drink it. I keep thinking I should go but don't get up. After his second cup he remembers food. He pulls things out of the fridge and I offer to help but he tells me to sit. My body is all out of whack. I don't remember this kind of silence with Jay. I don't remember ever wondering what to say or noticing any gaps. I miss him then, for the first time since we broke up. I ask Sam how he and Yash got the house and he says they'd been coming over here for dinner since freshman year when they had Gastrell for Late Medieval Lit. That's how Yash and Sam met, in that class. Gastrell got Yash a research job at the Sparrow, Sam says. Whatever that is. And, Sam says, he lets Ivan use his study in the faculty club.

'He's just really generous to his students. It's too bad you never had him for anything.'

I'm a good student in English. I get A's and A-'s and nice words at the bottom of my essays. But I've never made friends with any of my professors, all men except for Iyengar. No one has ever given me a perk or suggested a seminar. I waited on Professor Wyler at High Five once, I'd had him for Modern Poetry sophomore spring. He was alone and drank three bourbons and asked me what time I clocked out. I don't think he was planning to tell me about the honors program. If I'd had Dr. Gastrell, maybe I'd have gotten to see his green bedroom, but I doubt he'd have given me this house for the year for nothing.

Sam makes toast and eggs over easy. He sets the plates down on the table with a ketchup bottle and I feel heavy as lead. I force myself to take a few sips of the black coffee.

I hear Yash coming down the stairs.

'What's for breakfast, good people?' he calls before he comes in. Somehow he knows I'm still here. 'Morning. Morning.' He stands at the table, looks down at our plates. 'No, no, no. How many times must I say it?' He removes the ketchup and replaces it with red and orange and yellow bottles from the fridge. 'You must never let Sam make you eggs. It is an exercise in Baptist blandour.'

'That's not a word. Even in French.'

'Blandiosity. Blanditas.'

I pick up the yellow and the orange and sprinkle a few dots on top of the fried eggs. Yash grabs the third bottle and splashes red all over them. The labels are faded and I can't tell if the sauces are from India. Sam told me Yash's dad had come to this country alone from Delhi when he was nineteen. He said that Yash's dad liked to say he stepped off the plane and the first thing he did was get the craziest girl in Tennessee pregnant.

Sam and I watch Yash make his breakfast. He bounces around from fridge to sink to stove. He puts a kettle on and I'm relieved when he replaces my coffee with a cup of tea. He sits down between us, on the side facing the wall, and starts eating fast.

He looks up after a few bites. 'Sorry. I eat like a jackal.'

'Older brothers?'

He shakes his head. 'Only child. But my mother needed to clean the plates as soon as she served the food. You have siblings?'

'A brother. And steps.'

His eyes widen. 'Divorced parents. Yay.' He looks at Sam. 'Two heathens against one saint.'

He definitely knows what happened in the bedroom.

Sam takes his plate to the sink. 'One of her parents might have died, Yash.'

Yash looks at me.

'Divorced,' I say.

'Evil stepmother?'

'Satan's sister.'

Sam stays at the sink, rinsing his plate for longer than it takes. I've known a number of religious people and for a while my mother took me to Mass because she was in love with the cantor, but I've never known the kind who sleep with Saint Augustine and Saint Paul by their bed. Sam pours himself another cup of coffee. Number four.

Yash sees me notice. 'I hope you can stomach the smell of that stuff.' He looks at Sam. 'Can I tell her?'

Sam shakes his head weakly.

'Do you know the Valkyrie?'
'Who?'
'Valerie Hayes?'
'No.'

'Sam's old flame. Coffee made her gag. He stopped drinking it for her and he was a beast and that's a whole different story, but one weekend Sam's parents came into town and took us out to a lovely brunch and we're eating our benedicts and Sam's dad takes a sip of coffee, leans a little too close, and Valerie spews up her eggs so fast no one has time to duck. No one is spared.'

'It wasn't that bad.'

'It was that bad.'

'My parents loved her.'

'His parents loved her. Even after that. Good people. Good country people.'

'Shut up, Rooster.'

'They're a tad religious.'

Sam pants. 'A tad.'

'A speck. Sam is the rebel. Can you imagine? This is what a black sheep looks like in the Gallagher household.'

Sam is unreadable, looking down into his coffee cup.

'I have to go,' I say. 'Unlike you overachievers, I haven't even started Dryden's essays.'

My sweater is upstairs by the bed and I think about leaving it, but my mother knit it for me in high school.

I go upstairs. Sam's in the hallway when I come back out with it. I can hear Yash clanking things around in the kitchen. Sam puts his hands under my shirt and slips them down the back of my jeans. He tastes like the coffee percolator and moves me back into the bedroom. He shuts the door. We don't make it to the bed. We slide down to the rug and I have my back against the door and he pulls off my jeans and his tongue isn't on me for more than half a minute before I come and he rocks me with his hands beneath me and does not take his mouth off me and I come some more and I can hear the door banging a bit and I try so hard to be quiet but I can't do anything but let it out.

He was very good at that.

'You're very good at that,' I say.

He grins up at me. 'There are some advantages to abstention.'

'You really haven't had sex?'

He doesn't answer.

I know I should ask more questions but I reach for the button of his jeans—no belt today—and he doesn't stop me.

Everything but, we used to say in high school. Sam and I get really good at everything but.

Carson and I share a room in a house with eleven other people. We pay forty-four dollars in rent each month. There's no heat and at the end of November we all pitch in and buy a large propane gas heater we call Mavis and keep her in the living room. To be warm in that house in winter you are either asleep under blankets or draped over Mavis. I start spending more and more nights at the Breach House—Dr. Gastrell named it after D. H. Lawrence's childhood home—where there are tall radiators in every room that crack and sizzle with real heat. Utilities are included in their free rent, so they keep the thermostat cranked. The first time Carson comes over she cannot stop talking about the temperature. She sheds layers, piles them on an armchair. 'I feel like I'm going to get malaria in here.' She strips down to a T-shirt and twists her raised arm around. 'I have not seen my elbows in weeks.'

'You don't shower?' Sam says.

'God no. You can't shower on Pye Street in winter. You would die. I shower at the gym.' Carson was on the volleyball team. 'Fast. All my teammates want me.' She flashes Sam her big smile.

I take her upstairs.

'It's even hotter up here. Jesus.'

'Don't take the Lord's name in vain in this room.'

She looks at the bed. 'So this is where you don't fuck.'

I shush her.

She looks at the books on the bedside table I've told her about. 'It's not going to end well.' She shakes her head. 'But the heat.' She flaps her bare arms around. 'I get it.'

Ivan teaches us a new card game called Sir Hincomb Funnibuster that some girl from Connecticut taught him. He removes the fives, sixes, sevens, and eights from the deck and with the remaining cards explains that each suit is a family, every king the head of his family: Spade the Gardener, Club the Policeman, Heart the Lover, and Sir Hincomb Funnibuster, who is the king of diamonds. The remaining cards are different members of each king's family. The first person to collect a full family wins. All the cards are dealt out and the only way to obtain cards is to ask another player for one, but each request has to be spoken with the exact same polite phrasing, and you must say thank you before you touch a card someone gives you. If you mess up, the first person to scream 'Sir Hincomb Funnibuster!' gets your turn.

'Sam?' Ivan says.

'Yes.'

'May I please have Spade the Gardener's twins?'

'Yes, you may.'

Sam slides the two of spades across the table.

'Thank you,' Ivan says, but too late, after he touches the card, so we all scream 'Sir Hincomb Funnibuster!' as loud as we can. Then we argue about who started screaming first.

You have to pretend you're not looking for the suit you want, and you're always trying to disrupt others from getting what they're looking for. There is ganging up and subterfuge. We all have our tics and tells. I always ask for the parrot—the three—of the suit I'm pursuing. Sam always asks for the eldest son. Ivan never learns to say thank you before touching the card he's asked for, and Yash always forgets about the donkey. Sam cannot scream 'Sir Hincomb Funnibuster' without leaping up and knocking things over. When I scream, Yash says my eyes look like they're going to pop off my face like buttons.

It's deeply satisfying to win that game, to fan out a whole family before anyone else does.

In bed that night after a few hours of Sir Hincomb and then our celibate sex, Sam tells me about his relationship with Valerie. She was Baptist like him, very pious, he says, and made it clear on their first date that she would not have sex before marriage. They fell hard in love and were together for months until they lost control one night and did it. He covers his face. 'We prayed, we went to each other's ministers, we stopped receiving the sacrament. But it ruined us.'

I do not say, you ruined it by believing in this man-made bullshit. I say, 'You were in love. It was a natural impulse.'

'I will never forgive myself for that. For doing that to her.'

'Sounds like you did it together.'

'It was my fault.'

'Why?'

'Because it's always the man's fault.'

'Why? Did you rape her?'

He glares at me.

I laugh. I'm incapable of understanding his dilemma. It feels completely made up to me. I've noticed that about people who had stable childhoods. They like to create their own problems.

'Why couldn't you apologize to each other, just say oops, that was a mistake, and move on? Isn't the whole point of Jesus about forgiveness?'

'We tried, but . . .' He struggles for a while to find the words, then says, 'We are all our sins remembered.'

'What the fuck, Sam. That's *Hamlet*, not the Bible. And it's a load of crap.'

He's angry after that and rolls over and won't speak. After he falls asleep I go back to my freezing house. On Monday morning he walks me to Modern Furniture like nothing happened.

My favorite nights are staying in and helping Yash pick out a shirt for a date, seeing him off, making dinner with Sam, and watching a movie or reading until Yash—and often Ivan—come back from their dates and tell us everything.

Ivan is all about Ivan. 'I was tremendous,' he says after an encounter on a waterbed with a med student. 'She'll never have it better than that.'

Sam laughs. He doesn't judge their behavior, though Yash doesn't seem to be having any sex at all. He comes back a lot earlier than Ivan and makes every evening sound like a complete fiasco. He takes a lot of girls out but never the one Sam says he has a real crush on. Lara Mertens. She's Austrian, with an accent so mild you have to listen closely for it. She was in a Japanese history class with me a few semesters ago, very stylish, a little sad, putting up with all the Americans. They call her the goddess. She doesn't seem right for Yash. I can understand the appeal—the beautiful skin, the pouty disdain, the tailored jackets—but she doesn't look like she has any fun. He's so sharp, so quick, so eager to make a fool of himself. He needs someone who gets him entirely.

A few weeks before I met Sam, a girl I knew had been killed off campus, stabbed to death, the school paper said in the only article they wrote about it. No one I knew knew her. Carson had gone home for the summer and I'd cobbled together a few sublets before we moved into Pye Street together in September. In August I ended up in Franklin Terrace for a few weeks and so had she, this girl from Iran. She was going to be a sophomore and took summer classes during the day. I was working at High Five at night, so we didn't see each other much. I only remember a few real conversations. She told me her father had worked for the Shah and they'd left Iran when the Shah did, nine days after the start of the revolution, when she was nine. She had the most delicate and pale skin I'd ever seen, as if a ray of sun had never touched it. She had a crush on the boy in the apartment next door. He was going to be a sophomore, too. When she told me he'd asked her out, she leapt around the apartment like a deer. She was a virgin, she told me. She'd never had a boyfriend before. We lived together for three weeks. I don't remember saying goodbye. She wasn't there the day I moved out. I didn't see her on campus after that. A month later she was dead. That boy's roommate had raped her and stabbed her sixteen times in the apartment next to ours. I heard the news on the college radio station the morning after it happened. I went to the funeral alone. I didn't talk about it. But sometimes I woke up in the dark in Sam's bed and thought of her—Cyra was her name—and her small upturned nose and that tender skin.

One day in January, after we've come back from the holiday break and our schedules are all different, I go over to the Breach thinking Sam will be there, but I find Yash alone, smoking a pipe in the study.

'Is this what you do when no one else is home?'

'It is. Sam doesn't think we should touch them. He says they're antiques, but it just makes you feel so'—he holds the pipe by the bowl and takes three exaggerated squint-eyed puffs—'Lord Mountbatten.' He opens the drawer. 'Here. Sit. I'll fix you up.' He lifts an ivory pipe from the holder, stuffs it with tobacco, lights it, and passes it over.' This pipe has a spectacular downward curve to it. The stem is a little wet from where Yash put his lips.

'Do you inhale?'

'No, no, I don't think so.'

We puff together and laugh at our poses.

Then he takes the pipe out of his mouth. 'I need to tell you something, Jordan. I feel like I should have somehow mentioned it sooner.'

I stop puffing too.

'I was at the funeral. For Cyra. I saw you there. I recognized you from class and I wanted to say something to you—you looked so upset and you weren't there with anyone—but I didn't and I'm sorry. I was there because I knew the guy who killed her, and I didn't want to tell you that.'

'You knew him?'

'His older brother was on my hall freshman year. The police found a sweatshirt with my name in magic marker—my mother labeled all my clothes in magic marker—in that guy's apartment. His brother must have swiped it from me and he ended up with it. They questioned me about him and I didn't know why, then I saw the article in the paper.'

'The one article.'

'Yeah.'

'How did they keep it so quiet?'

'I don't know. Because she was foreign, probably. How did you know her?'

I tell him about the sublet and everything I remember about her. He listens and his face looks like it did while he was sleeping. The grandfather clock strikes three. Sam will likely be home soon. I follow Yash to the kitchen and we wash out the pipes and put them back in their rack.

I want to say more about Cyra but I've run out of memories. I barely knew her. 'Are you religious?'

'No, I don't think so. I'm something, but it's not religious.'

'Spiritual?'

'Maybe.'

'Seeking?'

'Somewhat. A weak seeker. Not for God or gods, though.'

'Sam wants me to read *The Confessions of Saint Augustine.*'

He smiles.

'You've read it.'

'It's sort of required reading to be his friend.'

We hear the latch of the gate outside. We move quickly from the study into the living room.

Sam comes in the door.

I'm on the couch, Yash in the chair opposite. I call out a hello and Yash says, 'We're in here,' and neither of us sounds like ourselves.

Sam doesn't notice.

'Hey.' He drops his books on a side table and sits beside me. 'No one told me how boring Stubbs is.' He makes a face. 'It smells weird in here.' He sniffs me. 'You smell gross.'

Yash and I look at each other. 'We tried out the pipes,' he says.

Sam shakes head. 'You both reek.'

'I feel sort of sick,' I say.

'Me too.'

'Children,' Sam says.

In February Sam and I drive down to his parents' house outside of Atlanta. They are kind, serious people and though they call him Sam Bam most of the time, they take his life very seriously. I can't quite believe the attention they give him, the questions not about what classes he's taking—they already know his whole schedule—but whether he decided to write his take-home essay on Cicero's 'De Fato' or his letters to Brutus, and if he was still having trouble with Hume. His mother has a new pillow for him because he had mentioned a crick a few weeks ago. The crick was from a strange position we'd gotten into, but he doesn't even give me a side glance as he accepts the gift. Sam's younger brother and sister barely speak. They behave like the governor has come to lunch. I'm given the guest room off the living room. Sam will sleep upstairs in his old bedroom.

That first afternoon Sam is tired from the drive and says he's going to go upstairs to take a nap before we go to some neighbors' for drinks, then on to dinner at a new restaurant nearby. I'm not a napper and I'm definitely not welcome upstairs. I read on my guest bed. At five thirty I stick my head out into the hall that leads to the living room and hear no sounds. I don't know what time we're expected for drinks but I start getting ready. I change into a dress and tights and new gray boots I'd gotten for Christmas. I'm putting on a little mascara when there's a knock and the door swings open.

'We've been waiting for you for a half hour,' Sam says. 'What are you doing?'

'I've been waiting for you to come down and get me.'

'Why didn't you come out?'

'I did. No one was around.'

'Because we were all waiting for you in the foyer.'

'Well, I'm sorry I didn't know to look in the *foyer*.'

When we join the others, I assume Sam will explain the situation. He says nothing.

'I'm so sorry,' I say. 'I didn't know you were waiting.'

Their smiles are thin and they move quickly to the car.

I feel self-conscious about the mascara. I only put it on because I was bored, waiting for Sam. And they think I've held them up deliberately because I was primping.

When his father orders coffee after the meal, I promise him I won't projectile vomit, but no one laughs.

It's a bad visit from start to finish.

Back in the car the next day I think we'll laugh about all the terrible moments, but Sam finds nothing about the visit amusing. He's angry. He thinks I've been disrespectful and impertinent.

'Impertinent? What am I, six?'

'If the shoe fits.'

'How was I impertinent?'

'The things you think are funny are rude. "I promise I won't throw up." Why would you bring that up? Why would you want to humiliate Valerie in front of my parents?'

'I was not humiliating Valerie, because Valerie was not at the table.'

'You were mocking her in absentia to elevate yourself.'

'I was just trying to break the ice *in presentia* to add a little humor. It was all so stiff.'

'It was stiff because you threw everything off schedule. We were late to drinks, late to our reservation.'

'Because you did not tell me when we were leaving!' We'd already been round on this ten times by then.

'Why didn't you come out of the room?'

'Why didn't you come get me? Were you not even allowed to touch the door of the guest room in case I lured you with my sexy wiles into mortal sin?'

His list of complaints is long: the mascara, the tall tight boots, holding the door for his father, cynical jokes, revealing that my father was fired from his job. 'You create unnecessary drama.'

'At least I didn't say what he got fired for.'

'Please don't tell me.'

I tell him he is a prude in the very worst sense of the word, the most incurious, self-righteous, unchristian sense. He basically says I'm an unwashed heathen who seeks attention through my embarrassing depravity. It's a brutal fight and we say awful things in that car. We drive through some snow flurries, light flakes that don't stick on the windshield and have stopped falling by the time we get back to school. I ask him to take me to Pye Street but he won't. He wants to keep fighting. When we get to the Breach it's empty—Yash has gone up to UVA to see a girl he went to high school with—and he grabs me and presses me against the front door. Soon our clothes are pulled down and fueled by the fury of our fighting we have sex, real sex, right there in the hallway on the bare floor, the little table with the notepad teetering above us.

Sam seems fine about it afterward. We bring our overnight bags upstairs and we go down again and make some sandwiches and sit on the couch with our schoolwork. He reads Horace and I read Whitman. He makes coffee and brings his cup into the living room and says, 'I am glad it doesn't make you vomit,' and we laugh and I lean against him and we keep reading. It's very quiet, without Yash coming in to say he's making some popcorn or a pot of tea. I wonder how his weekend at UVA is going, if he and the girl from high school are more than friends. I'm a hundred pages behind for tomorrow, but the words swell and I realize I've fallen briefly asleep.

'I'm going to go up,' I say. 'I'm beat.'

Sam lowers his book. It takes him a moment to look up at me. 'Could you,' he says, rubbing his thumbs along the edge of his textbook, 'go home?'

I go upstairs and retrieve my things, everything I ever brought into that room. My bag won't zip and my backpack bulges. At the top of the stairs I look at Yash's door, partly open. If he were here I'd start crying. But he isn't, so I teeter down the stairs with my bags and go straight out the door without a word. Sam doesn't come after me. It's started to flurry again. On the sidewalk I can see him through the window on the couch. I don't know if he's pretending to read or actually reading. After a few minutes, after he thinks I've walked away, he lifts his face toward the window. He looks scared, like something out there is more menacing than the snow falling faintly, faintly falling on the living and the dead.

The house on Pye Street has gotten colder and my twin bed feels smaller and Carson's snoring is a bit more piercing. Different people live here now. Athletic Joe has been replaced by Irish Maxwell, and PhD Jenny had dumped her fiancé and begun a needy, gropey relationship with sports medicine Caroline. They've sealed the windows with blue plastic to conserve heat so there's an aquarium feel to the place during the day, but you still have to vie for a spot around Mavis in the frigid mornings. Maxwell and Caroline are recovering from religious childhoods and reassure me that I've done the right thing by walking away and being through with that lubberwart, as Jenny, who is getting her doctorate in Medieval Studies, calls him. On the phone my mother tells me he has a Madonna-whore complex.

'All men have it,' she says. 'His is a little more pronounced.'

'Maybe he's just being honest?'

'There's nothing honest about the degradation of women. It's a power move and it's been working for a few millennia.' She's a better feminist than I am.

She sends me an orange sleeping bag with a little hood for my head and it's cozy. I mention to her that Carson uses it when I'm in class and she sends one to her, too. She has lived on a tight budget since the divorce, but that has never impeded her generosity.

I don't run into Sam on campus, but I pass Yash once in the crowded corridor of Tate Hall between classes. I spend the rest of the day analyzing the nature of his surprise at the moment he saw me. That night I lie in my sleeping bag and feel sad that he can't be my friend now. I'm aware that I had ideas about the future that I hadn't discussed with myself. I figured Sam and I would go on separate paths after graduation, but I hoped Yash and I would stay friends, that we'd be friends for life. Now that seems a lot less likely. And this is the thing I'm most sad about.

Sam comes to Pye Street eleven days after he told me to leave. He hands me a short letter and watches me read it. It is dry and unspecific for an apology. At the bottom he has signed it 'Heart the Lover' and that makes me smile. He kisses me before I can speak and, after a talk in my freezing bedroom, we go back to the Breach, where Yash and Ivan actually woo hoo when I come into the living room.

The next morning is Sunday and Sam goes to church. He hasn't gone since I've known him. He told me he didn't like the new minister. But last night he said he was going to give him another try.

When he gets up in the morning I keep my eyes closed. I'm not sure how I feel about being back in the green bedroom. I was giddy playing Sir Hincomb last night. I faked them all out and ended up getting two full families, which none of us had ever done before. Yash made me a crown out of a pizza box and Ivan pulled me up and spun me around the room. In bed Sam and I tried to talk and we tried to cuddle but those weren't our strengths together. The talk involved a lot of fancy footwork around the fact that he thought we had both sinned in that brief moment in the downstairs hallway and I did not. We didn't have actual sex after that, but it came closer than you'd think given our animosity and all our avowals not to.

I hear Yash go downstairs. Ten minutes later the house smells of sautéed onions and garlic and I know he's making hashbrowns to go with his scrambled eggs. If I get down there quick enough he'll make enough for me.

The potatoes are crackling in the cast-iron pan and he doesn't hear me come down. I stop in the doorway and watch him scrape and flip with a spatula. He's got on gray sweats and a fraying blue Allman Brothers T-shirt. His hair is wet, the front part in a great loop high above his forehead. This is why Sam and Ivan call him Rooster, this way he has of drying his hair. I've never seen it before.

I don't know how to not startle him. 'Mmmm,' I hum softly. 'Smells yummy.'

He jumps. A few potatoes fly off the spatula.

'Jesus, Jordan. I thought you guys went off somewhere.' He looks mad but also very funny with his hair looped up like that. He sees me see it and I see him stop his hand from trying to fix it. 'It's not funny. My heart is going a hundred miles per hour.'

'I'm sorry. Here, you sit.' I pull out a chair for him. 'And I'll stir.' I take the spatula from him. He actually does as he's told. When I turn around again he's tousled his hair back to normal.

'Sam go to church?'

I nod. 'Should I scramble some eggs?'

'Sure.'

'You do the cheese,' I say and fetch him the cheddar and a grater. We are used to cooking together. Sam is happy with a PB&J and Ivan only likes takeout. But Yash and I cook chicken legs and fresh vegetables. I often make my mother's picadillo and he makes his grandmother's butter chicken. But we've never been alone in the kitchen together for this long. We've never cooked for two. I crack the eggs into a bowl and froth them with a fork. I divide the potatoes on two plates then pour the eggs into the pan and scrape up the browned bits of potato and onion into the scramble. The eggs don't stick, and cook quickly in nice chunks, not pebbly like they get in the cheap frying pan on Pye Street. I sprinkle on the cheese just before taking them off the flame.

'God, those look perfect,' he says when I bring them to the table. He's set it with green cloth napkins I've never seen before.

'This is so nice,' I say, sitting at my place across from him.

We both look at the clock at the same time.

We take a few bites and compliment each other on our parts of the meal, then we eat quietly. It isn't the kind of silence Sam and I have, where each of us will say something if we can think of it. With Yash I can say anything and it will turn into a conversation. We could talk about the green napkins—where he'd found them, what they remind us of, who ironed them—for a half hour. But I want to make it count. I missed him during those eleven days. I thought we couldn't be friends anymore. I can't say that but it's all heavy in my mind. We have less than a half hour before Sam comes back. We need to talk about something big, something that will secure our friendship forever. It's a lot of pressure to put on twenty-five minutes on a Sunday morning. I glance over at him when he's putting both eggs and potato on his fork with a knife. He eats in that British way his father must have taught him, the knife so active, not just for cutting. He has a very small smile on his face, as if he doesn't notice we're not talking, or as if we are.

He catches me looking at him and the grin spreads. 'Glad you're back.'

'Me too. I missed this place.' I look around the room, as if that's what I missed, then point to a copy of *The Inferno* on the counter and ask what class it's for.

'It's not for a class,' he says. 'I'm just doing a little advanced reading for Gastrell's Immortality seminar in the fall.'

'The fall? You're not graduating with us?'

'I took a leave of absence sophomore year so I have another year.'

Sam told me that he'd taken time off. He said Yash's dad had put his mom in a psychiatric hospital and Yash'd had to get her out. I asked how Yash's dad had had the power to do that when they'd been divorced since Yash was five, and Sam said he didn't understand why I wanted to be a writer when I could never just trust a story.

I like that I'll know where Yash is in the fall. 'Have you read that story "The Last Fall" by Ray Hart, about a guy who stays at college for an extra semester?'

'Do tell. The plot sounds positively riveting.'

'It's beautiful. All his friends are gone and he sees the back of the neck of an old girlfriend in class and marvels at the feelings he once had for her and he's got this housemate who only plays an album called *Country Greats* and the leaves are falling and the cold is coming and he has this thing with another girl that's not really serious but there's this gorgeous moment next to a soccer field when she fastens and unfastens a button on his jacket.' I can't read the expression on Yash's face. 'It's just this long tender farewell to youth.'

'I'd like to read it,' he says, and nothing else. No quip, no barb.

'I haven't done it justice.'

The back door rattles and we both jump. Sam is in the window. He gives the door a shove with his hip and it comes unstuck. I've never seen anyone go in or out that way before.

He comes in and plucks at the green napkin in my lap. 'Fancy.' He spins around to the stove and studies the skillet. 'None for me?'

Yash and I both get up and start chopping onions and potatoes. Sam pours a cold cup of coffee from the percolator.

'How was church?' Yash says.

Sam sits in my seat at the table and stretches out his legs onto Yash's chair. 'The new guy hasn't gotten any better. Everything is in the interrogative, like he is seeking and questioning *with* us. It's such a pose.'

'Maybe he *is* questioning,' I say.

'If he is, he shouldn't be in that job. God is not a question. He's the answer.'

Yash and I are shoulder to shoulder at the large cutting board with our knives. I want to give him a quick glance, but Sam in this twitchy mood might catch it. Instead I tap my knife two times without cutting anything. Yash taps twice back.

After he eats, Sam and I walk to the library. Yash goes to study with someone named Annabel at the bagel shop. Sam takes my hand and pulls me off the path and against a tree and we kiss for a while before moving on. This attraction is our only language, and it's fading. Still, after that it's hard to focus on *Cosmos* for astronomy, a gut to fulfill my science requirement. I watch Sam instead. We always sit at a table in the library, not in the armchairs near the windows where I used to sit before I met him. He has a book pinned open with his left hand and writes swiftly in a notebook with his right. He's translating Ovid back into Latin, a poem called 'Iphis and Ianthe' from *Metamorphoses*. I looked down at my paperback. It really is like we go to different schools. Next he'll move on to Early Modern Ethics. He's got Hume, Rousseau, and Kant stacked up beside him. Since I lost my golf scholarship, my college education has been funded by a series of loans and my job at High Five. I am going to have to pay it all back, this paltry dabbling I've done, these wasted years. I haven't been serious. I watch how quickly Sam writes in Latin.

He looks at me. 'What's going on?'

'I've made all the wrong choices.'

\* \* \*

I go to my advisor. He teaches courses on Swinburne that I've never taken and is always adjusting the back pillow behind him. He shaves, but he lets the hair grow wild everywhere else on his head, great tufts sprout from his ears and nostrils, his eyebrows are thickly entwined.

I tell him I want to do an honors thesis in creative writing.

'Too late for that,' he says.

'I want to stay another semester.'

'It'll mean another loan.'

'I know. I want to write an honors thesis and take two seminars.'

'You have to have a pretty high GPA for those.'

I hand him my transcript.

His tangled eyebrows move around. He removes the pillow behind him and replaces it with a smaller one beside his chair, then hands me back my transcript. 'So be it,' he says, and does something with his mouth that I think is meant to be kind.

A few weeks later, I run into Yash outside my writing class. It's midafternoon, early March, the sun strong again after its brief winter waning. Sam is in his Ethics seminar for three hours. Yash and I walk toward the quad. He says he was planning to get an iced tea and read in the sun. I say that was my plan exactly. He remembers that my story was being workshopped that afternoon and asks how it went.

'Everyone was very nice about it,' I say.

'Even Bryce?'

I laugh. I told him once about Bryce, a guy in my class who had no tolerance for female protagonists. If a story was about a woman, he would inevitably say that he'd had a girlfriend like that once. I don't think he realized how often he said it. 'He didn't say a word.'

He bumps against me briefly. 'He loved it!'

We get teas at the cafeteria and sit on the steps in the sun. I have this feeling that this is how all of college should have been and somehow wasn't, sitting with Yash on the steps of the quad. I have a stab of sadness, then I remember.

'I'm not graduating either.'

'Really?'

I tell him about the thesis. I don't mention the seminars I've signed up for. One of them is Immortality and I don't want him to think I'm stalking him.

He nods and doesn't say anything else. I point to the copy of *The Golden Bowl* by his foot and ask how it's going and he tells a story that his professor had told him that morning about how Henry James, upon hearing of the writer Constance Fenimore Woolson's suicide, went directly to her apartment in Venice, destroyed his many letters to her, and tried to drown her dresses in the lagoon, but they wouldn't sink. Yash acts out this story with much élan, gripping the gondolier's pole James used to push the gowns underwater and recreating his haunted face as they floated back up to the surface. Yash is even-keeled, always in a good mood, but today there seems to be an extra bit of joy. When he's done he sits back down and puts his face up to the sun. 'I'm glad you're staying here,' he says, not opening his eyes. 'I'll have one friend.'

'Me too.'

He bumps me with his shoulder again. 'We'll have our farewell to youth together.'

I tell Sam that night after my shift at High Five, so that he hears it from me first. We're on his bed, eating jellybeans from the Easter basket his mother sent him. He has a stronger reaction than I anticipated.

'You like to make things hard for yourself, don't you?'

I shrug my shoulders. Here comes the judge.

'You gave up your scholarship and took out student loans that everyone knows are hard to pay back even when you have a real profession in mind. And now you want to rack up another semester's worth of debt—for no good reason apart from the fact that you don't want to grow up.'

I was still in my work uniform: khakis and a teal polo shirt with a basketball decal high on the left boob.

I'd worked every semester of college, and two jobs during summer. Sam had worked part-time at his father's office in the summers and, after a trip to Europe this coming summer, that's where he'll work in the fall.

I look around at his free house with free utilities. I lift up the pink Easter basket by its handle and swing it between us. 'I'm not sure you want to go toe to toe with me on growing up, Sam Bam,' I say and get a small smile out of him.

The deadline for Sam's and Ivan's theses looms. Ivan got all his anxiety out early and now puts his head down and writes the thing, while Sam, who expressed no concern about it all year, is suddenly a wreck. He's writing about Hume's principle of contiguity, but finds himself beginning to disprove his own argument. His coffee intake triples, he starts smoking, and the only way he can fall asleep, for the few hours that he sleeps, is if he lies on his stomach while I rub his head and sing. The first song I sing to him is 'Scarborough Fair,' which reminds me of 'Been Too Long at the Fair.'

'Do you only know songs about fairs?' His voice is muffled, his face mashed into the mattress.

'Maybe.'

He is asleep before I can start 'North Country Fair.'

The singing lasts for a week or two. He says I have a pretty voice and calls me Calliope. I wonder if Yash can hear me from his room. After he hands in his thesis, he slowly calms down. He asks me to help him quit smoking. Cigarettes had killed two of his grandparents and he promised his parents when he was a boy that he'd never touch them. He has to be free of them by graduation, he tells me. I make little bundles of cigarettes tied with ribbon for the next five days that reduce his consumption by three each day. On day six, no more.

A few days before graduation we go to a senior dance. Yash got up his nerve and asked Lara Mertens. We meet them there. The party is outside and there's a band and a bar and blazing torches sunk in the ground all along the edge of an enormous garden. Lara is friendly. She kisses me on each cheek, asks me if I've read any more Japanese history and rolls her eyes. When Yash speaks, she is very attentive. She likes him. Yash is not himself. He has a sort of mask around other women, I've noticed. I thought maybe with Lara it would be different but it isn't. Other friends come up and we get separated from them and at some point Sam tells me to stop looking at Yash and Lara.

'I can't tell if he's having a good time.'

'Of course he's having a good time. He's on a date with the goddess.'

I run into a couple of people from my writing classes and talk to them for a bit, then I see Sam bum two cigarettes off his friend Brent. I excuse myself and walk over and pluck them out of his pocket. He tries to grab them back but I clutch them tightly and in our struggle I get knocked hard to the ground.

It's a semiformal. I'm on the ground in a pale green dress. I see Brent's disgusted expression as he looks down at me. He doesn't have time to hide it. He doesn't offer a hand up. Sam does, but I don't take it. I get up, brush the dirt off the back of my dress, and walk directly out to the road and the two miles home to Pye Street.

I don't go to graduation. I work brunch and dinner at High Five and get out at midnight. My housemates are having a party. I have a beer on our porch and take their ribbing about having not actually lived there this year. Carson is the only one leaving. Starting in June I'll pay eighty-eight dollars a month to have the room to myself. I tell them they'll be seeing a lot more of me now. I leave Carson and Jenny making out on the porch swing, which surprises me and makes me feel the distance between us. I haven't been around enough lately for her to tell me about this development. I go to my room and feel the floor shuddering from the music and the dancing in the living room where Mavis used to be. I stand at my window looking out at the street, watching the steady stream of students and parents come down the hill from campus toward town. The parents try hard to blend in and some of them are just as drunk and keyed up as their kids, but their bodies move differently. I wouldn't have asked either parent to come and they wouldn't have offered, and I see now that that would have been painful, not to have family here this weekend. I doubt I'll stay for the ceremony in December, so I won't have to deal with it. Not graduating now was a good decision all around.

I stand there for a long time. I recognize a few people under the streetlamps: Mark from my psych class sophomore year, Ryanne and Landry who lived on my hall last year. Then I see Brent and another friend of Sam's named Cole—and Yash. He walks slightly behind. I haven't seen him since the semiformal. I don't know how it went with Lara. I think about opening up the window and yelling out to him but instead I pull back a bit. What was he like with other people, not me and Sam and Ivan? He's never been here, probably doesn't know which house I live in. He's talking and the other two are laughing and I wish I could hear what he's saying. When he's alongside the house he looks over at the people on our porch, then directly at my window. I stay still. I don't know what he can see. He moves on.

Carson leaves with her family the next morning, a three-car caravan back to Brooklyn. I hug them all on the sidewalk, Carson the longest. Jenny comes down the steps with a coffee cake just out of the oven. I'm surprised by their tears. We wave them off and I go back to my room. It feels enormous, and empty. Only now can I see how absent I was for our senior year. We moved in at the end of August and it was roasting hot and we lay on our twin beds cooling ourselves off with ice cubes, talking and laughing before sleep. We'd lived together starting sophomore year. She knew everything about my family, kept track of every detail even though she never met any of them. She had a mad crush on my brother. She didn't care that he was gay. She said once that if she ever met my father, she'd kick him in the balls. Her family came to visit twice a year. Her parents had gotten pregnant with her in eleventh grade and her father freaked out and fled to Texas and her mom had the baby and mailed him a photo. He was at the door less than a week later, pleading for forgiveness. Their parents helped with Carson, they finished high school and got jobs, bought a home, and had four more children. They were much younger than Carson, her siblings, and they worshiped her. They'd come screaming out of the car and glom onto her. They stayed in our room, all four of them fighting about whose turn it was to sleep on the bed with Carson. This past August, when they'd driven her down, the youngest, Meg, had asked if she could sleep with me. I scooted over. She told me I smelled good—she did not, she smelled like burnt licorice—and fell asleep nine seconds later.

August feels like a decade ago. I try to retrace the year. I remember mornings before class. We ate our cereal together on the porch, those warm September mornings. We had a '70s party at the house the second week of class and blasted Earth, Wind & Fire and Queen. The cop who came after the neighbors complained sat with us on the porch and told us he wanted to be an astronaut. We drove with Joe and Caroline to Hatteras for a weekend. We threw the Halloween party. And then a few mornings later my clock radio alarm went off to the college station and the news that Cyra had been killed.

'I know her,' I said.

'Know who?'

'Listen.' I turned it up.

Carson fades after that. Everything dims a bit. What happened? I went to the funeral. I met Sam. I met Yash. It got cold.

I get back into bed. Carson and her family will have reached the highway by now. It's eleven thirty in the morning. I'm tired to the bone.

I come home that night to a box on my porch filled with things I left at the Breach: a few T-shirts, *Cosmos*, a hairbrush that's not mine. At the bottom there's a note from the little notepad by the door, folded in half.

> I'm sorry about our fight—we both can be pretty stubborn sometimes. I'm taking off in a few hours. I guess we've reached the end of our road. What a long strange trip it's been, no? Yash's dad called a while ago and he asked how my love life was going. I told him and he said that

Jordan sounds like the kind of girl you divorce. I know you'll take that the wrong way. However, it helped me to see we didn't have to be together. I didn't have to fight for some polysyllogistic fallacy of my own making.

    Don't forget to graduate someday!

                        Cura ut valeas,
                        Sam

I've never burned anything anyone has written to me in my life, but I take that note straight to the gas stove. I light it and watch it curl and blacken in the sink. I wash the flakes of ash down the drain.

Still, the words reverberate. *Jordan sounds like the kind of girl you divorce.* What hurts the most is that it's probably true. I've never known a happy marriage. My mother was miserable and left my father for the cantor, who seemed like a good guy, but he died before they could marry. I don't think she's had a relationship since. My father married Ann, a neighbor who stood by him when he got fired for drinking with the high school boys he coached and showing them the peepholes in his office that looked into the girls' locker room. He treated Ann worse than my mother. My brother said recently that Ann had called him from the closet where she was hiding from him. She wanted to know what would happen if she called the police. She didn't want him to go to jail.

I probably am the kind of girl you divorce.

At least Sam is gone. I don't know if Yash has left yet for Knoxville for the summer. I walk to the library. It's empty. All those seniors who packed the place last week are gone forever. I find 'The Last Fall' by Ray Hart in an old *New Yorker*, make a xerox, and walk to the Breach. Yash's car is still there, his bedroom light on. I go quietly around back, slide the pages under the kitchen door as far as they'll go, and flee.

Two days later his car is gone. There's a wheelbarrow filled with soil in the driveway, two fat azalea bushes wrapped in burlap beside it. The backyard has been mowed and the air smells sweet and like the past.

I apply for a new loan and get a few dinner shifts at Chantal, the most expensive restaurant in town. Only six tables and no entrée under fifteen dollars.

After my first night of training there, I walk home and pass the apartment building where I lived for those three weeks with Cyra. I stop and identify our door on the second floor. It bothers me how little I remember, how distracted I must have been. How unfriendly maybe. She was alone. Her friends from freshman year weren't back yet. She never put anything in the refrigerator. I remember that. All that was ever in there was the stuff I brought home from the restaurant in the afternoon in aluminum containers with cardboard tops. Did she even know how to cook? Did I ever offer her my leftovers? The place looks like a cheap motel, with its balcony that stretches the length of each floor. There are people outside partying in different spots. It must have been like that last summer when I lived there but I don't remember it that way. This must've been where she met that boy next door, and his roommate, out on the balcony. It feels like one of my jobs, to remember her. How had the university buried her story? I remember she leapt like a fawn across our living room.

I stand there a while, then head toward home. At the foot of Pye Street is a laundromat called Bubble Time. I stop there next and look through the windows. It's a funky place with good music and a café, indoor and outdoor seating. The walls are psychedelic colors and the machines are painted, too, each one a different animal. You feed your clothes into the mouth of a lion or an orca. I've heard it's hard to get a job here. They pay over minimum wage, and there are tips from the café plus the tip jar at the register that's always overflowing. Supposedly the couple that owns it sells drugs from the shed in the back parking lot.

It's quiet when I go in, two people reading on a couch and the owner—Lorna—beside the register. She doesn't look up. She's swirling a paintbrush around in a glass of green water. When I get to the counter I can see her painting, a centaur holding a piece of fruit—a female centaur, with long hair, bangs, and breasts.

'That's lovely,' I say, because it is.

She looks up at me.

'Are you hiring?'

She holds her paintbrush up like she's outlining my face. 'Sure. Why not?'

Bubble Time is where I meet Claudette. Claudette is an incorrigible flirt. She's most of the reason for the stuffed tip jar. There are always guys hanging around long after their laundry is done. Her other job is at Häagen-Dazs. I meet her there when she closes at eleven and we eat mounds of ice cream, lock up, and go to Don't Answer, an outside bar with picnic tables and kegs along the fence. With Claudette you always met a guy, a fellow sidekick. I dance with them on the hardpacked dirt and go home alone. I like my room on Pye Street. I push the beds together and keep a stash of books beside me and read late into the night and early in the morning. I start reading *Don Quixote* for Dr. Gastrell's seminar in the fall. I take notes. I write a short story, only five pages, the first one I've written that was not for a class. I like it. It has a different flavor somehow. It feels entirely my own.

There's an oversized astrology calendar on the wall behind the counter at Bubble Time. Inside each day's box are suggestive planet positions like Wet Venus in Aquarius or Sextile Jupiter in Scorpio. I flip past June to September 3, a Tuesday, the day I would have the first class with Yash. Mercury–Saturn Square, it says, unsexily.

I keep my eye on that calendar. I note the day Sam flies to Barcelona. He is gone. He's left the country. Claudette and I go to Don't Answer that night. They're only playing Prince, and everyone gets up on the picnic tables for '1999.'

The next morning there's a note pushed through the nail on my door:

*Yash called*

I can't call him back. I don't have a number. He said he was going to live in his father's barn for the summer. I could call information for his number, but I'm not about to call over there. *Jordan is the kind of girl you divorce.*

The only reason Yash would try to reach me would be something to do with Sam. A plane crash, a Eurail accident, a nightclub fire. Something awful must have happened to him.

I'm at Bubble Time when he calls again. Michael, Lorna's husband, waves the receiver at me. 'It's a boy,' he whispers loudly.

My stomach lurches. I reach for the phone.

'Jordan,' he says, with a little laugh that acknowledges the weirdness of his tracking me down.

'Yash.' I plug the other ear with my finger to block out the music. I brace myself. I don't know what's coming. 'What's up?' I can hear the alarm in my voice.

'Well, I'm—' There's a small crash in the background. 'Shit. Catastrophes abound. I was thinking. I was wondering. I can't find a job here. I thought maybe I'd come back there. I have a couple of leads on a sublet but I'm wondering if—for just a night or two—if there might be a couch free on Pye Street?'

My lungs feel hot and tight. Michael is wolfing down an enormous platter of nachos and watching me. I clench my eyes shut. 'Yes, there's a couch. We have a couch. It's yours.'

He asks if tomorrow is too soon and I say it's great. Then I say I have to go because my very stoned boss is glaring at me.

'I wasn't glaring,' Michael says after I hang up. 'I just thought I might have to go get my defibrillator for you.'

'You know he's never going to sleep on that sofa,' Claudette says later, when I'm stuffing our filthy couch cushions into our biggest machines.

'It's not like that.'

'Do you know how much you talk about this guy?'

'It's not like that for *him*. And even if it were, he wouldn't. He never would.'

'Right.'

She squats down behind the counter. I can hear her rifling through Michael's stacks of CDs. She switches out the disc and 'Jessie's Girl' comes blasting out of all eight speakers.

'No, no, no,' I say but she pulls me out near the door where there's space and makes me dance with her.

\* \* \*

The next afternoon I get off work and run up the hill. His car is there, his mom's old red Chevy Nova. I touch it. It's real. He's here.

I climb the porch steps slowly. I hear Dylan playing through the window. I see the back of his head. He's on the freshly cleaned couch, my housemate Maxwell in the beanbag chair. I listen at the screen door. Low rumbly talk about *Blonde on Blonde*. He's wearing a shirt I've never seen before. His hand is on his knee, his long fingers thrumming along. He is in my house. Dylan is singing about Johanna.

I step inside.

He jumps up.

'You found the couch.'

'I found the couch.'

'Good drive?'

'Good drive, yeah.'

We don't hug. Maxwell watches our awkwardness. He has no plans to leave the room.

'Thank you so much for this.' He looks at Maxwell. 'It will only be a night or two.'

Maxwell grins. 'Uh huh.' Maxwell slept on this couch for three months until a room opened up.

'You hungry?' Yash asks. 'Should we get some dinner?'

I change out of my work clothes into my favorite summer dress, pale blue with big white buttons down the front. We've never had summer together. I force myself to breathe.

Then we're in the Nova. I'd been in it a few times, Ivan up front, Sam and me in the back. We'd gone to a party in the woods somewhere. Another time we went to a barbeque restaurant in Raleigh. Now I'm in the passenger seat and Sam is in Europe and Yash looks over at me.

I want to tell him about Willie Sylvester. He asked me out at recess in sixth grade. I'd had a crush on him since third. 'I feel like I'm in a dream,' I said to him when he asked me. I feel like that again, in the passenger seat of Yash's car.

'Where to?' he says.

I suggest Cate's because it is a few miles out of town and I remember him saying once that they had the best bread pudding he ever tasted. He looks relieved to have a destination, puts the car in gear, and pulls out slowly. The Nova is at least fifteen years old. The smell, the seat fabric, the pebbly vinyl dashboard remind me of being little.

'Did you grow up with this car?'

He smiles. 'You can hear my mother screaming, can't you?' He switches into a piercing Deep South accent. 'You know what I think? I think all y'all are lazy butt bums!' He clenches the wheel and narrows his eyes at me then lifts himself up close to the rearview. 'The three of you. Three lazy bird turds.' He puts his eyes back on the road and pretends to swat everyone in the car.

'Who were the other two?'

'Arlo and Bean. They lived across the street. She yelled at them like they were her own. I was always with them.'

I ask if he saw them when he was home and he says that Arlo was working on an oil rig in Mississippi and Bean dropped out of school to manage a band called Stationery. 'They're going to be bigger than Toto, he told me, and I said, who the fuck is Toto, and he went crazy. I still don't know who Toto is and no one's ever heard of Stationery, but Bean says they're getting traction in Japan. I have this scar on my lip'—he leans over to show me something I've seen a hundred times—'because in fourth grade I said "Fly Like an Eagle" was a terrible song. He pushed me off my chair in homeroom and my front tooth went clean through. Oh shit, here we are.' He turns into a dirt driveway.

Cate's is a farmhouse. All the lights are on. He shuts off the engine and turns to me like he has no plans to get out of the car. 'Who were your neighbors?'

I tell him about Mrs. Kane, her whispery voice and frizzy white dog and how she wrote books my mother wouldn't let me read. 'I tried to anyway, but they didn't have them at our library.'

'We'll have to find them.'

'We will.' I look at him, then look away. I'm scared he'll see how happy I am.

## HEART THE LOVER

We walk up the farmhouse steps. It feels like a date, like something we've done many times with other people over the past few years but never with each other. We don't speak until the hostess asks us if we are two. We follow her to a small corner table on the back porch. It's overlooking a flower garden. The plants have just been watered and the air is humid, dense with the smell of the roses and phlox below our feet.

A waitress comes over with a pitcher of tea. She takes a book of matches from the pocket of her apron and lights the little candle in the glass holder in the center of the table. There are no other students here. Everyone around us, including the waitress, is decades older. We aren't going to get interrupted or seen by anyone who knows Sam. It's just us. I have him all to myself. I take little glances of him looking at the menu, his thick hair falling across his forehead the way he likes it, his scarred lip. I'll never touch him. I know that. I don't know what Sam has told him, but even if he believes Sam and I are truly broken up for the last time, he won't cross that line. He wouldn't be here if that were a temptation. There are plenty of other people he could have asked to stay with. Once I think all this through, I relax. It's not a date.

The waitress takes our drink order and leaves us alone in our corner on the porch. We look at each other and laugh.

I start to ask him what happened back home and he says at the same time, leaning in, 'I was the one who pointed you out to Sam, you know.'

'I thought it was when my stupid Bacon parody got read out loud.'

'It wasn't supposed to be a parody. "Contemporary imitation," that was the assignment. But yours was a parody.'

'I couldn't help it.'

'It was very funny.'

I take all the credit. I don't say that it was the professor who made it funny.

'It never occurs to me to be funny in writing. I always get so grim.'

'But you're such a funny guy.'

'I know it.' He widens his eyes in bewilderment and we laugh.

'So that wasn't why Sam noticed me?'

'No, it was a little before that. And I noticed you. First.'

I look back down at the menu. I'm worried my blushing is making me sweat. I take a sip of the iced tea then blow into the glass and the air comes back cool on my face.

The waitress returns with two beers and takes our order. I hand back the paper menu quickly, hoping he doesn't see it shaking.

'So what happened back home?'

He shakes his head. He doesn't want to talk about it.

'Weren't you going to work for your uncle at the paper?' His uncle Percy works at the *Knoxville News Sentinel*. He told me once that Uncle Percy was like George Willard from *Winesburg, Ohio*, a newspaper man with big dreams stuck in his hometown forever. But when Yash gave him the book and suggested the similarity, his uncle said, 'You're way off base, son.'

'Yeah, I just couldn't do it. I didn't want to be there.'

I thought there'd be more of a story.

He tells me he got a letter from Ivan in Dublin. 'His first line was "I've seduced the landlord's daughter."'

'Don't tell me. He was incredible.'

'Yes, he was. Off to Poland next, in time for the election.'

The elections in Poland are a source of contention on Pye Street. Solidarity is poised to defeat the Communist Party and possibly leave the Eastern Bloc. 'The Marxists in my house are not happy,' I say.

'Marxists are never happy. There's never quite enough purging or mass graves for them.'

'Hungary could be next. Do you think it's possible that it will all just collapse?'

'And the wall comes down and everyone, even the Marxists, live happily ever after?'

'More happily, at least.'

'Maybe. For a little while. And then some new force will appear to make them miserable again. We're not exactly improving as a species.'

'Yes, we are.'

He laughs. 'No, we are not.'

'How can you say that? All of literature rests on the promise that we change, we grow, have epiphanies, become better, understand our flaws.'

'Too late. Have you ever noticed that? It's always too late. Oedipus, Macbeth, Raskolnikov.'

'For them. But not for us. We have gotten better. Ethically. Morally.'

'We haven't. Human behavior doesn't change.' He is so certain of this.

I insist it does and give the obvious examples of the spread of democracy, the abolition of slavery, increasing religious tolerance, women's rights.

He counters with Hiroshima and Nagasaki, the Gulag, Vietnam. More people have been killed in this century in wars and by their own government than in all previous centuries combined. If killing another person is any measurement of ethical behavior, he says, we are worsening. I argue that it is the technology of war that has changed and that the majority of people have a wider sense of fairness and a belief in freedoms, and perhaps these wars are more ethical than the ones in the past that were for land and lucre. 'You don't think these wars are for lucre? Yes, cultural norms and fads bring temporary progress here and there, but that's not a change in human morality. Inside we are all exactly the same as we have ever been and will always be until we extinguish ourselves soon enough. To believe otherwise is just a story you tell yourself to sleep at night.'

'I don't think I could live without a belief in moral progress.'

'And I can't feed myself lies. There's a lot of beauty along with the pity and fear, as Aristotle said, in it all. Our famed condition.'

'Is that what life is to you, a tragedy?'

'Of course it's a tragedy. A very silly one. The absurdity is as great as the despair.'

'No room for hope?'

'Not much.'

'I wouldn't want to live without hope.'

'Well, I do. I like it here.'

We realize the waitress is stalling in the doorway with the dessert menus.

She moves toward us. 'I didn't want to get in the middle of anything.'

'We were having our first fight,' he says, looking down at the choices. 'Arguing about whether humans as a species are improving or not.'

'Oh yeah? Let me guess who's the Pollyanna.' She points to me.

I raise my hand in confirmation.

'That's a keeper, hon,' she says, patting Yash on the shoulder as she walks away.

We study the desserts.

If Sam and I had this conversation, he'd ask for the check and not speak on the way home. But Yash looks up and grins and asks me if I like bread pudding.

Back in the Nova he says, 'Where to now, Pollyanna?'

I don't want to go home. I don't want the night to be over. When the night is over he'll find a job and a sublet and I might not see him till September 2nd. 'Don't Answer?'

This surprises him. He smiles and starts the car. We pull out onto the road back to town. He is driving slowly. When we crawl up to a deserted intersection, he comes to a full and very long stop.

'Okay, Mr. Cautious,' I say. 'I think you may proceed.'

He chuckles. He likes to be teased.

We park and walk down the little alley to get to the back of the bar. The music blares. Elvis Costello's 'Welcome to the Working Week.'

'I haven't been here since freshman fall.'

'Let the farewell to youth begin,' I say.

He stops and looks at me. 'That story,' he starts to say, and the rest is drowned out by Claudette, who is screaming my name. She comes running up, beer sloshing out of her big cup.

'Yash! You're Yash,' she says and I lean back so he can't see me and glare at her to tone it down. She gives me a wicked little smile then hugs us both and tells him very loudly and way too close to his ear that the couch cushions are very very clean. 'Come, come,' she says and grabs our hands and leads us to her group by the fence.

'Hey you,' a guy named Billy says to me as we pass his table. Another, Cody, points at me and says, 'We're dancing to Guns N' Roses tonight.' All the sidekicks are here.

Yash is amused. 'Well, Miss Popular certainly hasn't been at home moping. Can I get you a beer?'

He goes off to stand in one of the keg lines. Claudette grabs me and pulls me down onto a picnic bench with her. 'That guy is in love with you.'

I don't believe her, but all my muscles weaken anyway.

'I wish.'

'Trust me. He is.'

'Nothing can—'

'Oh, I *know*. Nothing can happen because he's such a *good guy*. Good guys are human. He just needs a signal from you.'

I put my head on the picnic table. 'I'm not good at signals.'

'I know. That's what's so cute about you. But in this case you'll have to give him one.'

I rock my head back and forth.

'A small one.'

'What's going on?' Yash says, back with three beers in a precarious cluster.

I straighten up.

He squeezes in on the other side of me. It's tight. Our sides are touching and I feel him trying to not press too hard against me. He's cooler than I am. How do I give him a sign when I can't breathe? Another beer is only going to make it worse. Unlike the rest of the population, I get more awkward with alcohol. I put the cool plastic cup against my cheek.

'Have you ever spent a summer down here before?' he asks.

I shake my head.

A guy named Buck and two Seans are vying for Claudette's attention. She leans over me and grills Yash about why he came back from Knoxville, where's he's going to look for work, and who was from India, his mother or his father? Her questions reveal how much I've spoken to her about him. I'm relieved when Buck interrupts and we start playing a game that involves placing one, two, or three fingers at the edge of the table. I think they must have been playing it earlier because everyone understands how to play but Yash and me. One of the Seans shouts the rules to us but they make no sense.

'Uno, dos, tres, fire!' Buck says.

Fingers go on the table. Yash and I both put out two.

Buck looks at all the fingers. 'Crack crack,' he says to me then to Yash, and he bashes our fingers with his fist. It stings and we laugh. We play many more rounds and no matter what we do we get cracked every time and we're laughing too hard to figure it out.

The song 'Africa' comes on.

'It's Toto!' I yell at Yash and we all get up to dance. He's a very cute dancer. I didn't know this. The way his hips move, his body still boyish. I can't quite take my eyes off of him. He looks happy. His hair swings loose. His smile is enormous. 'This is the stupidest song I've ever heard,' he says.

'Give him a sign,' Claudette says.

I shake my head.

'What did she say?' he says.

'I couldn't hear her.'

He doesn't believe me but he's still smiling.

We dance to Madonna and Roxy Music. One of the Seans takes Claudette's hand and pulls her in close as if it were a slow song and says something that makes her laugh a long laugh. This is the Sean she likes.

Brent and Cole come through the back alley. I haven't seen them since the semiformal.

Yash glances in their direction and puts his lips close to my ear. 'Should we go?'

The house on Pye Street is dark when we pull up. I don't want to go in. There will be no sleeping for me, with him downstairs on the couch.

We walk up the porch steps. 'I didn't know what to do, after the senior party,' he says.

'What was there to do?'

He gets to the top step and sits. 'I didn't know what happened.'

I sit too, but not close, not where I want to. It would have been an easy sign, to sit closer. 'You and Lara were inside.'

'We came out and you were gone.'

'I'd wanted to go in but Sam said I should leave you alone. And then—it doesn't matter. My biggest regret is not getting to hear how it went with you and Lara.' It occurs to me that maybe Lara is still here, maybe he's come back for her.

'She wasn't my type.'

'Really?' The relief is instant, buoying. 'After all that?'

'After all that. I didn't know what to do after you left. I was so angry at Sam for not going after you, for not apologizing. He never apologized, did he?'

'No.'

'He felt shitty about it, he did. But he couldn't say he was sorry.'

'He was angry about a lot more than cigarettes.'

'I know.'

But I don't know what he knows, what he means.

'He wrote me a note. You probably know that.'

'I didn't know that.'

'It wasn't an apology. It was more of a screw-you.'

'I'm sorry.'

'It's fine. He wasn't my type.'

'I could have told you that last fall.'

'I wish you had.'

'I knew about the first note he wrote you.'

'Oh yeah?'

'I might have helped him a bit. At the end.'

'Heart the Lover?'

He smiles.

Fuck. 'That was the only good line,' I say. 'You were quite the puppet master.'

'I didn't mean to be.'

'You salvaged our first date, too. "How was the daisy?"' I say in a loud voice.

He laughs. 'I didn't think he'd get you back there after *The Deer Hunter.*'

'Three hours straight of Russian roulette.' I put my finger to my temple and pull the trigger. 'Click.'

'I told him it was a bad idea.'

'I've never felt this way about anyone and I know he's your best friend and I don't wish him ill, but I honestly hope I never have to see him again in my life.'

'I'm assuming this means you've broken up.'

I laugh.

He shrugs. 'I didn't know for sure. Things were tense before he left. He wasn't himself. Then he did leave and I wanted to go see you but I didn't know if you'd want to see me or if you'd think Sam had sent me, that I was doing his bidding or something. I started to think I wouldn't even have one friend left in the fall and then that morning just before I left town, I saw the story at the back door.'

'You liked it.'

'I hated it.'

'What?'

'Maudlin, overwritten, banal.'

'Banal?'

'Isn't the whole thing about writing that the stakes have to be high? Who cares about this dope wandering around campus?'

'That moment at the end when they're standing there and—'

'I know, the button thing. Didn't do it for me.'

'It was gorgeous and tender. Everything in it is working toward this mood, this ache, this very tactile sensation that gets deep in your bones. He sort of reminded me of you.'

'Of me? That loser? How does he remind you of me?'

Because I'm a little in love with him. Because he moves me. I can't think of anything true that I could say out loud.

'If I ever write something decent,' he says, 'it's going to be a whole lot better than that.' He stands up. 'Hold on. I have something for you.' He goes quickly down the stairs in the shirt I hadn't seen before today, his skinny arms, his dark elbows. He reaches into the back seat of his mother's car. He comes back up the stairs and hands me a book. 'Sorry. I didn't mean to arrive completely empty-handed.'

It's a paperback, gold and black. *Hunger* by Knut Hamsun.

'It's about being a writer, no matter the cost.'

'Thank you.' I want to hug it. Instead I read the back. Or pretend to. The words won't stay in place.

'I was nervous earlier. So I forgot to give it to you. You'll like it, I think.'

'Why were you nervous?'

'I wasn't sure you really wanted me here. That you were just being nice. On the phone.'

'Wait till you sleep on that lumpy couch. You won't think I was being very nice.'

'And I worried you thought it felt like a date, tonight. At the restaurant.'

I laugh. 'It did feel a little like a date, didn't it?'

'You put on a dress.'

'I did.'

'And the waitress thought so. She called you a keeper.'

I love that we're reminiscing about the evening already. But for some reason I blurt out, 'Your dad said I was the kind of girl you divorce.'

This stuns him.

'Sam told you that?'

I nod.

'My dad has said that about every woman since he left my mother. Even my stepmother.'

I'm embarrassed I brought it up.

'My dad is a jerk, Jordan. It's why I couldn't stay there. He didn't want me working for my uncle, he didn't want me seeing my friend EJ. He didn't want me spending time with my mother or playing tennis. One minute I'm a lazy hippie and the next I'm a pretentious yuppie. Either way, he's convinced I am an all-American fuck-up, which is sort of his catch-all for any kind of person except him. I'm like my mother, I'm as useless as a beggar in Calcutta. Just a running commentary. He has these things on repeat and one of them is that every woman is the kind of woman you divorce. I feel awful you had to hear it.'

I wish I hadn't said it and need to change the subject. 'Have you ever brought a girlfriend home?'

'Never.'

'Not even Megan.' That was his girlfriend in high school.

'No. Only my mom met her.' He tells a funny story about Megan causing a small house fire with her curling iron and I tell him about the foyer fiasco in Atlanta and we are comfortable again.

We go in the house and I show him the kitchen. There aren't as many dishes in the sink as normal and I fear it is giving him a false impression. 'There's one bathroom and it's up here.' He follows me up the stairs with his Dopp kit in the dark. 'It's disgusting,' I whisper.

Outside the bathroom I tell him he can use it first.

'Oh, okay. Thank you. Noche noche, then.'

'Noche.'

I turn around and go into my room. I can't bear to shut the door all the way. The bathroom door shuts. I stand there. I take off my underwear and throw it in the hamper. It's soaked through. My whole being wants one thing, the one thing it can't have. The clock radio says 3:33. I had nine hours with him. Why isn't it enough? Nine hours ago we were talking about Arlo and Bean and Mrs. Kane. I think of something and laugh out loud.

He's in the doorway. 'What's so funny?' he whispers.

I go closer to whisper back. 'I remembered this Halloween when we rang Mrs. Kane's bell and she had no idea what day it was and gave us all old cough drops from the bottom of her purse.'

He kisses me.

'I'm sorry,' he says.

He kisses me again. 'I'm so sorry. I want to know more about Mrs. Kane. I do.' He walks me backward a few steps into my room. We kiss. 'Oh my God I've wanted to do this for so long. You have no idea how long.' We kiss a long time. He looks over my shoulder. 'This entire room is bed.' He looks at me again. 'Am I bungling everything? You should probably tell me to go downstairs right now.'

I shake my head.

He lifts his hands to the top of my dress. 'I have thought about doing this all night.' He unfastens the first button and looks at me.

I nod but before he can undo the next one I pull the dress up over my head and toss it in the corner. I'm not wearing anything else.

He is kissing me and laughing. 'You didn't let me do the whole sexy button thing all the way down.'

'Claudette told me to give you a sign.'

'This is a good sign. I love this sign.'

We get his clothes off, too, and we are still standing, looking at each other and grinning.

The feeling catches me off guard.

Oh.

Love.

Yash never did look for a sublet. We bought king-sized sheets for the pushed-together twins and I raced home at night after work to join him on that big bed. Every night was hot and we slept without clothes or covers, our bodies close, our skin steaming. He got a job as a prep cook at a diner two doors down from High Five and if our breaks lined up, we'd meet out back and make out.

For my birthday in July he brings me breakfast on a tray: scrambled eggs, sausages, a biscuit, and a little fruit garnish like at the diner. My mother has sent me a package and after breakfast I open it, a thin cotton bathrobe that goes on then comes off quickly. He climbs on top of me and slides inside and we move together. I'm watching him, watching his face start to flush, start to lose control of its expression, and he looks down at me watching and it seems like he's in pain when he says, 'I love you. I know it's too soon, but I do. I love you so much.'

We don't just have sex. We read *The Aeneid* out loud to each other. We read Yeats and Auden. We read Proust in French because we both studied it in high school and we talk about moving to Paris. But Proust in the original is difficult, and we'll read him in English in Gastrell's seminar in the fall, so we read Camus in French instead. And we make up a version of Sir Hincomb Funnibuster that you can play with two people. It's like honeymoon bridge, he says, which I've never heard of. Honeymoon Hincomb, we call it. Then we start calling each other Hincomb. Then Hinkie. Then Hink.

In early August I have to have my wisdom teeth out. My teeth are so impacted that the doctor has to crack apart all four teeth and take them out in pieces. I chose local anesthesia so I am awake for the whole thing. Afterward my mouth aches and bleeds but I don't care because Yash, after a trip to Claudette at Häagen-Dazs, comes dancing through the door, a pint in each hand, singing 'Strawberry Sorbet' to the tune of 'Raspberry Beret.'

Ivan comes back from Ireland and stays with Brent for a few days. Before he comes over, Yash moves his bag and books back out to the living room.

'Brent's futon is a lot better than this,' Ivan says to Yash when he sits on the couch.

'It's only a few more weeks.' He's found a room to rent for the school year.

We go to a diner. Yash and I sit on the same side of the booth, knees touching under the table.

Ivan tells us tales about Bloomsday in Dublin, about meeting Joyce's grandnephew in a barber shop in Mary Street. 'At the barber's, man. Like Buck Mulligan shaving on the roof. 'Twas mystical. What? What's going on? You guys have not stopped laughing since we got here.'

Then he tells us about the landlord's daughter, the ferryman's sister, and a pretty French girl on the flight home who told him in a sexy accent if they didn't hold hands during takeoff the plane would crash. 'Best come-on line ever. I'm using that one.' But once they were safely in the air she let go and refused to speak to him for the rest of the flight.

He is amused that everything he says delights us. 'Whatever you guys are on, I want some.' he says, which only makes us laugh harder.

'Sam should be getting back soon, right?' Ivan says to me.

'No idea.'

'He hasn't been in touch?'

'We broke up before he left.'

'Heard that before.'

'Definitively this time. Very mutual. Fini.'

Yash presses his leg against mine.

'Ça suffit?' I say.

'Yup, we got it, Hink,' he says and we freeze.

'Hink? You two have gotten super weird,' Ivan says.

The next night Yash goes out with him alone while I'm working. He comes back later than me and flops on the bed. 'The guy has no clue. Picked up on exactly nothing. This might be easier than I thought.'

'To hide it forever?'

'Not forever. I just want Sam to hear it from me first.'

The week before classes start, he moves into his room on MacDougal Street. It's bigger than mine, the bathroom is cleaner, and there is AC. It's like going to a hotel. I stay there many nights in a row.

One morning, early, the phone in the kitchen rings. One of his housemates knocks on the door. We've been messing around. 'Please don't move,' Yash says.

He comes back so grave I think his father has died. 'Sam is coming for the weekend.'

We leave no trace of me in his room. He borrows a mattress and I help put the sheets on it. We sleep separately that night. Sam is coming early the next day.

I work lunch at High Five and an evening shift at Bubble Time. I jump every time the phone rings, hoping for an update. He was planning to tell him straight off, get it over with. By nine I've heard nothing. Claudette wants me to go out, but I can't risk running into them. I go home. Yash is in my room, sitting stiffly on the bed.

He looks at me and shakes his head.

'What happened?'

'He got here and I showed him my place. We went out for lunch. I knew you were at High Five so I took him the long way around. It was bad. Even before I said anything it was bad. I kept feeling like he knew. But at lunch he talked all about some girl he'd met in Berlin, and then about you and how the breakup had been for the best. And I'm thinking, this is going to be fine.' He laughs. 'I'll just tell him and it will be okay. But I can't seem to do it. We go over to see Cole and have some beers with him and that guy Lonnie from Pike, and they're both surprised I've been in town all summer and haven't come by or been out at the bars and as we're walking out of there Sam asks me if I'm seeing anyone. And then I'm sure he knows. Maybe Ivan did say something? Shit, I don't know, but I say it.'

'What did you say?'

'I said I'm thinking of taking Jordan out.'

'*Thinking* of *taking me out?*'

He drops his face into his hands. 'It's all I had the courage for. And he flipped on me. Said I could never ever do that, that it would be reprehensible, unforgivable. He told me to swear to him that I would never do that. And I could not. I have no idea where he is now.'

'Maybe he went home to Atlanta.'

'No. He's here. He's not through with me.'

'You're going to have to tell him the truth.'

'I know.'

I walk him downstairs. Hug him at the door. Watch him move slowly up the hill to MacDougal Street.

I have the house to myself. Everyone else is out. I knew Sam would react that way. Yash will lose him if he chooses me. I will lose Yash if he chooses Sam.

I'm in the bathroom when I hear knocking at the front door.

'Jordan,' he calls.

He must have followed Yash here. Fuck. I move slowly to my bedroom. The light is on, the window open. I sit on the floor so he can't see me. The knocking continues. The door is unlocked. He doesn't come in. I hear steps going back down the front porch.

'Jordan.'

He must be standing directly below my window.

'I just want to talk to you.'

A long time later he walks away.

I don't hear from Yash for the rest of the weekend. On Sunday evening he comes into Bubble Time with his laundry. After he gets a load going, we sit together on the patio. He reaches in his pocket and pulls out a small figurine made of blue glass. He gives it to me. It's a dolphin, back arched, about to surface for a leap.

'It reminded me of you.'

'I didn't take you for a tchotchke giver.'

'It's an aberration.'

'That bad?'

He nods. 'I told him. That it had already started. With us. It was bad. He was so angry. I get it.'

'You *get* it? When exactly does his owner's warrantee on me run out?'

He bends his head over so far I can't see his face. 'I don't know how to do this.'

He gets up and goes back into the building and out to the street and disappears. His clothes are still swishing around in the washer. I leave them there when my shift is over.

At home my bedroom door is closed and there's a note on the nail.

I'm in your bed. Wake me up so I can apologize all night.

— (the real)
Heart the Lover

Classes start. Dr. Gastrell's seminar is held not in 1B of Tate Hall as listed in the course catalogue but at his house. Every Wednesday night Yash and I walk together to the Breach, through the gate, up the little path, and ring the bell whose sound, to me, means the arrival of pizzas. We go through the hallway with the wobbly table and the notepad and the silhouettes on the wall. Yash and I sit together on the striped couch and a grad student named Vinga sits on my other side. Randy, a fawning junior, takes one armchair and high-strung Ned takes the other, his long, nervous legs stretched through the underside of the coffee table. Others bring in chairs from the dining room. Dr. Gastrell sits in the spot where Yash stood and acted out his date. Gastrell is fond of reading aloud. When we read *The Aeneid* he pauses on a line then reads it again: 'Someday we will remember even these our hardships with pleasure.'

Dr. Gastrell does not conceal how taken he is with Yash. Yash illuminates him. When he speaks, Gastrell shimmers with energy. They spar and parry about Platonic forms, Aristotelian ontology, and Homeric divinations versus human agency. Gastrell makes attempts to include the rest of us, and several of the others work hard for his attention, but the real conversation is between him and Yash while the rest of us listen and take notes. Their most heated dispute is over the definition of 'hamartia,' which Gastrell says is a tragic flaw. Yash corrects him, saying that the word in ancient Greek, as Aristotle was using it, meant a random error of judgement. From there it escalates quickly. Gastrell claims that nothing in Greek drama is random and that Greek drama wouldn't have survived at all without this tragic irony that they invented. Yash insists that the power and poignancy come from the very randomness itself, the sense that any one of us, not just a good king with a built-in flaw, is capable of making a mistake, that we are all vulnerable to tragedy because we are human.

The argument leaves Gastrell with a red neck and a moist hairline, and Yash looking like he slayed a small dragon.

For my thesis, I'm assigned an advisor I've never heard of and I meet with her every week. If there's any place I can point to where my writing life actually began, it is here with Dr. Felske on Thursdays at one p.m. I come in each week with two copies of a new story and have to read the whole thing out loud while she follows along on her copy, circling words, squiggling a line under sentences, slashing whole paragraphs. Very occasionally there is a tiny check in the margin. I write for these tiny checks. I get more and more of them as the semester goes on. She quickly understands how limited my reading has been, and how male. She feeds me Virginia Woolf, Katherine Mansfield, Zora Neale Hurston, Elizabeth Bowen, Djuna Barnes, Nadine Gordimer, and Jamaica Kincaid. By mid-November I've written twelve stories. We choose five for the thesis and begin to revise. Revision for me in the past has been some light polishing. This is more like a root canal on every paragraph. The writing professors I've had before often spoke in generalities, in quotes by famous writers. Chekhov said. Beckett said. And we scribbled down those pearls. Dr. Felske only talks about what she sees on the page. She taps her silver mechanical pencil on a passage. What is truer here? She steers me away from the Southern gothic plots I was enamored with last year and encourages me to write from my own emotions. I start to understand the power of fiction, the reason we make things up. My best story is about my father. It's not autobiographical. It's about the manager of a shoe store and the high school boy who gets a job there—but it is about my father, about my rage and shame and love for him. These scenes that didn't happen concentrate and distill the emotion of what did. 'The truth has nothing to do with the facts,' one of my professors said Faulkner said. Professor Felske shows me what that really means.

# HEART THE LOVER

\* \* \*

Madame Trèves, the owner of Chantal, comes slowly to like and trust me. It has taken four months. Once she starts telling you about her family, you're in, the bartender told me. On a slow night in late September, we are standing together in the little nook in back and she points to an old man she just seated. He resembles my uncle, she says, and I ask how and she says not his features, an energy, a goodness, and she tells me what I already knew from the bartender, that this uncle, her mother's sister's husband, hid her whole family in the hay shed on his farm for the last three years of the war.

The next week she gives me three more dinner shifts. I quit High Five and Bubble Time and start raking it in. Over a hundred dollars a night. I begin putting real money in the bank.

I bring home my tips and we count the cash on Yash's bed. I take a shower and when it gets cold I put on these red long johns I find in his closet. Your little red suit, he calls it, like in the Talking Heads song. We count my tips and roll around on the bed until the red suit is down at my ankles and never ever have I been so happy.

Every few weeks Sam comes to town and disturbs that happiness. He stays with Yash and I can't go to any of the parties they go to. My name is verboten. When they are together, I don't exist, Yash tells me. All their friends know not to mention my name. When Yash returns to me after the weekend, he doesn't want to talk about what they did or where they went or what they said. I hate Sam for this, the way he takes Yash away from me for days at a time and brings him back sullen and petulant and conflicted, the way I used to return to my mother after a weekend at my father's. I hate the smell of the room after Sam has been there. I hate the box of my things that Yash's housemate lets us store under his bed and that I retrieve once Sam has gone.

Once, in November, after one of Sam's visits, I don't go to Yash's on Sunday night after work and he doesn't come to Pye Street. The next morning I decide to do a little test, to see how long it will take him to come to me. I go to class, work on a story for my thesis in the library. Chantal is closed Monday nights. Yash and I usually get pizza. But he doesn't come or call. I don't hear from him Tuesday either. Or all day Wednesday. Gastrell's seminar is that night. If I don't see him before then, if I walk alone to the Breach and take my place beside him on the striped couch I will start to cry and not be able to stop. I skip my other class that day. I wasn't able to do the work. I know Yash has class till four.

I walk over to his house. I knock on the door even though I have a key. I feel like I've had a pot of coffee. My heart is going so fast. I'm barely in my body.

He opens the door. 'Hey, Hink!' It's confusing. He hugs me tight. 'Mmmm.' He presses his nose behind my ear. 'God, you smell good.'

We go into his room. He's gotten my box and put everything back where it belongs: my book on the bedside table, my brush on the dresser. He's been doing a lot of reading. There are at least a dozen books on my side of the bed. I'm trying so hard not to cry.

He opens the closet door and points to the long johns on their hook. 'I left the red suit out by mistake and Sam held it up and teased me and I thought for a minute he was going to put it on, so I grabbed it out of his hand and he said I'd turned into an asshole. It was kind of a bad visit. We saw at least five of your friends Saturday night. It was a minefield.'

He hugs me and kisses me and I can't speak and he doesn't seem to notice. 'I've missed you. Have you eaten? They had that cheddar you like at Kroger's.'

He goes to the kitchen and I have a cry in the bathroom. I want to tell him how I'm feeling, ask him if he noticed that we haven't seen each other since last Friday. This is what my old boyfriend Jay meant when he said I bottled things up. But I'm not good at saying that I feel hurt or forgotten or rejected. There had been no room for that growing up. I'm more skilled at burying those emotions. Or hiding them in my fiction.

I go back to his room and he brings me a sandwich and I can't stop the tears and he says, 'Oh, Hink, what is it?'

'I don't like it when Sam comes here,' is all I can manage.

He agrees that it's a tough situation and we lie down on his bed until we have to walk over to the Breach.

In December, when Madame Trèves helps me set the tables, I know something is wrong. She only helps when she wants to reprimand you. I'm not sure what I've done. She likes me. She and her husband had Yash and me over for Thanksgiving. We told her we wanted to write books and live in Paris, and she brought out boxes of photographs and told us about every arrondissement she'd lived in.

'You know you're my favorite,' she says to me, straightening the napkins I have just carefully placed.

'I am?'

She scowls at me. 'Of course you know that. And I don't want to lose you. I don't. But I make sacrifices. Not often. But I do. I have a niece in France. My sister's daughter. Two kids, no husband, and her girl just quit. Why she would employ a German I do not know. But she is in need. And you want a job in Paris. So there you go. A match made in heaven with me the only loser. You can write while the children are at school. Middle of January you go. You leave me.' She flicks me away with her fingers, insulted. As if it were all my idea.

On the way home to Yash's I think about Elizabeth Bowen's *The House in Paris*. I remember Dr. Gastrell saying that Ezra Pound invited James Joyce to stay with him in Paris for a week and Joyce stayed in the city for twenty years and wrote *Ulysses* and *Finnegan's Wake*. I think about how Dr. Felske is always talking about the two things that bring perspective and revelation to a character: time and distance. I think I have to go.

Yash is up reading. I tell him as soon as I'm through the door.

He is as surprised as I am. He wonders if I'll get paid enough, and if not, how I will defer my student loans.

I tell him I don't care about my student loans. 'How will they even track me down?'

He shakes his head. 'They will eventually, and the penalties will be harsh.'

Why are we talking about my loans? 'Will you miss me?'

'Of course.' He sees my face. 'A lot. Come here.' He scootches over on the bed.

I lie down next to him. I stroke his chest and he puffs it up, exaggerating the barrel of it, something I tease him about.

'I will come find you as soon as I graduate,' he says.

I want to go, though I don't want to leave him or our nights of honeymoon Hincomb and the little red suit.

He holds me tight and says until then we can write each other sexy letters like Henry Miller and Anaïs Nin.

At the end of the semester I skip my graduation and we drive to Knoxville. We don't stay with either of his parents. He doesn't want their scrutiny. We stay with his friends EJ and Marni.

I've heard a lot about EJ, one of Yash's best friends since elementary school. He and Marni started dating in eighth grade and when she got pregnant senior year they got married. Now they have a four-year-old and a two-year-old, and recently bought a house.

'EJ will be withdrawn when he first meets you,' Yash tells me in the car. 'Marni will do all the talking. Once we've had some drinks EJ will crawl out of his shell and Marni will let him shine. If you stay too long EJ will get morose, then belligerent. We'll slip off to bed before that. He's a good guy, but his demons are always circling.'

'Because of his dad?' EJ's father died of a heart attack in front of him when he was nine years old. He was the only one home. They were making hot dogs.

'I think he had them before that. Even as a little kid he always thought you were trying to rip him off. I think things were fucked up in his house. He complained about his dad, but once he was gone he was a saint. He always loved Marni. He was obsessed with her. It's good they're together. She's good for him. And those little girls. You'll love them.'

We pull into their driveway and the little girls come running and screaming out of the house, the littler one crying because she can't reach Yash first.

They call him Gas and he calls them the pigeons. He scoops them both up in his arms and they put their faces close to his and everything he says quietly to them makes them squawk and howl and kick their legs.

Marni is on the stoop and I introduce myself and shake her hand. She is our age, twenty-two, but I feel ten years younger beside her. She asks about the drive and I ask about the new house. She's watching Yash and her girls over my shoulder the whole time.

We all go in. We follow her through the kitchen to the living room with the pull-out we'll sleep on. The girls tug Yash into their room. She asks us to hang out with the girls while she finishes dinner. EJ will be home from work soon, she says. She's the first person my age I've ever met who has kids and a husband who will be home from work soon.

The girls want to make a fort out of the couch cushions and the blankets from their beds, and inside the fort they want to play a game called Prance, which Gas invented. It involves making your first two fingers do various movements and you have to guess the word for it.

'You can't do "prance,"' the older one says to me. 'That's the only rule. No prancing.'

Yash goes first and puts both fingers into the palm of his other hand and shoots one finger out straight before they both scream, 'Russian folk dancing!'

We all crack up. Yash says, 'I may have a slight advantage, having taught them a few concepts already.'

The younger one holds up her little palm and makes her fingers jump up and down. 'Jump,' I say. 'Bounce. Leap. Hop.' I wait for the other two to join me but they are smirking. 'Catapult. Gambol,' I say. The little one shakes her head.

'Saltate!' the other girl says then collapses laughing.

I could stay in this fort under these blankets all night. The little girls and their fat fingers and the words Yash has taught them. Everything is funny.

EJ follows the pattern Yash predicted. He becomes delightful halfway through dinner and he and Yash and Marni tell stories I've already heard but with fresh details. I don't want to get up and go to the bathroom in case I miss something. I never want to miss one single thing Yash says.

When Yash goes to the bathroom EJ says, 'He's never brought anyone home before.'

I nod, to confirm I knew this.

'No. This is a bigger deal than you understand.'
'EJ.'
'No, she needs to know.'
'What does she need to know?'

Something shifts in the way he looks at me. I have a volatile father, and I understand we've just made the turn Yash warned me about. Down the hallway the door to the bathroom opens. 'Do no harm,' EJ says in a low voice.

Yash recognizes the change and says he's beat from the drive and we quickly do the dishes and sneak off to the sofa bed, which is comfortable even when, by five a.m., there are four of us in it. By six we are up and on a walk to feed the horses at the end of the road.

We go to his mom's for breakfast. She's picked up seasonal work at a department store downtown and has to go in at ten that morning. She's so young, only eighteen years older than us. She has long hair and bare feet with purple nail polish and gives us both long tight hugs. This is the house where Yash was raised. He points through the window to Arlo and Bean's house across the street—'She's a doll but the husband is a waste of blood and bones,' his mom says—and at the Sullivans three doors down with nine children and the McDaniels at the end of the street with eleven. 'Big breeders on this street,' Yash says. 'My poor mom with her one strange Indian boy.'

She looks at him, displeased. 'Yashie. Don't say things like that.'

His mom has put out a big spread of food and he gives her a hard time about spending money trying to impress me.

'I wasn't trying to impress her. I just want to feed your bony self.'

We sit and he clams up and she talks about transcendental meditation and the tiny parking lot of the new market that has opened up. 'If you find a spot good luck trying to get out. It's tight as a tick in there.'

Every word out of her mouth annoys him. But she keeps trying. Even when it's clear she'll be late for work, she is offering us more food, coming up with new topics. Yash is holding up her coat and purse.

'You're gonna get fired, Peggy Lynn, if you don't hightail it right this minute.' He says this in a Deep Southern accent and I hear the boy he once was.

She gets up and lets him slide her coat on, hand her the purse and open the door. 'It was a real pleasure, Jordan. Hope to see you again, honey.'

From there we go to see his dad—*Jordan is the kind of girl you divorce*—for lunch. He and his wife, Paige, live on a farm thirty minutes outside the city. Yash always said his father left India far behind, but I didn't expect the ten-gallon hat or the slow Southern drawl. He works in whiskey. He owns a distribution company and it's all he wants to talk about: value chain, cost base, centralized buying, disintermediation, wallet share. The only time he veers from the topic of work is to tell Yash he knows about his mother's new boyfriend, Bud. 'That poor fellow has no idea what he's hitched his wagon to,' he says. Paige breaks in with many questions after that. He doesn't hide his impatience with these side conversations. Yash is humorless and docile. I don't recognize him. It's a great relief to get back in the car.

We spend the afternoon with his uncle Percy and his aunt Sue, who are easy and delightful. They are raising their little grandson, Jared, who loves Yash as much as the pigeons do. We eat pie at their kitchen table and play games with Jared in the yard. I watch Yash slowly unwind from the visits with his parents.

That night we cook dinner for EJ and Marni. The girls are our sous chefs. We urge their parents to go have some alone time in the living room but they stay at the kitchen table and watch us.

Late that night, after we've had stealth sex on the sofa bed, nervous the girls would bust in at any moment, we hear arguing. At first we can only hear EJ, low and forceful, but as he gets louder, Marni's responses become audible. She seems to alternate from combative to placating.

'Well, we avoided it,' I say. 'But Marni didn't.'

'I don't think she ever does.'

It stops abruptly a while later and the house is silent. Yash falls asleep. I stay awake a long time. Only after the girls crawl in beside me around three do I give in to sleep.

Yash drives me to the airport the next morning. It is early and we're quiet most of the way.

My hand is on his leg but his face is rigid and he doesn't look over. I wonder if he's angry I'm leaving.

'What's going on?'

He takes in a deep breath. 'I just wish I could keep driving, back to school. I don't want to be here for another week.'

'Come home with me.' I've already asked him. He's already said no.

He stops outside the terminal. He says they fine you if you get out of the car, so we say goodbye right there in the front seat of the Nova. I cry and he doesn't. He seems so far away, out of reach already, and that makes me cry harder. It feels like a mistake to leave.

'Hink,' he says, 'you're going to miss your flight.'

I pull my big suitcase out of the back of his car. I lean into the front and kiss him and I tell him I love him and he says it back, but he has disconnected. I shut the door and he pulls away. I wave and he waves though he is looking straight ahead.

\* \* \*

I fly to my mom's for the holidays. Yash and I talk on the phone a few times. Once he gets back to his place on MacDougal Street, he sounds more like himself. He says he's wearing the red suit and won't take it off until he gets to Paris.

The day after New Year's, I leave for France.

Madame Trèves' niece Léa lives at 16 rue de Vaugirard, two blocks from the Jardin du Luxembourg. There is a blue door, built for carriages, that clicks open with a code. In the entryway is a row of silver mailboxes. The poste comes twice a day, at nine in the morning and four in the afternoon. The family has started to call me le facteur, the mailman, because I check it so often for letters from Yash.

His letters are small packets, six to eight yellow legal pages of his small blue ballpoint print, full of observations, allusions, and reflections, perhaps more Henry James than Henry Miller, but with far more humor. I wait weeks for one. We are both broke and can't afford phone calls, though after three weeks without a letter I will break down and call him from a phone booth, my ten-franc pieces swallowed one by one. An hour's conversation is a third of my weekly salary. L'argent de poche, pocket money, Lèa calls it, because she is providing me room and board.

That spring, while he is writing his thesis, I do not hear from him for the month of April. I call twice and leave messages with his housemates on MacDougal Street and he does not call back. On the early-May day when Léa brings up the thick white envelope—she has met the real facteur on the street—I burst into tears. I run to my tiny room to read it. It is, as they always are, brilliant, erudite, distant, unapologetic; sweet and affectionate only in the last two sentences, like the turn at the end of a sonnet. 'Enough of my perambulations. I do love you, babe, cumbersome as it is for me to feel, and to confess.'

This is the first time he's used 'babe' on the page. It's his most tender endearment, which he uses only in the most intimate moments, when it feels like we are breathing from the same body.

At the bottom of this letter, in even smaller print, almost as a test to see how closely I am reading, is one more sentence:

P.S. I'll land in your land on the 5th of August.

I hoped he'd come in June or July, but it's okay—he is coming.

I need to start dinner, but I can't get a hold of myself. He loves me. He called me babe. He is coming in August.

Léa knocks on my door. She comes in, sees my tears, sits beside me on my bed. We've never been in my room together before. She's dressed to go out with her boyfriend, Laurent: silk shirt, suede belt, black skirt. She wants to tell me a story. She speaks in English, which she rarely does, only when she wants to be sure I understand every word.

She tells me that when she was nineteen she fell deeply in love. After a year he told her he wanted to go to the States, drive around the American West. He asked her to come, he begged her to come, she says. But she had to finish her studies. And her parents didn't want her to be an American hippie dropout. He left, and when her studies were over she didn't join him as she had promised. 'I don't know why. I suppose I was hurt he left. And then he met someone. He wrote me. I was écrasée. Completely broken. I could barely move. But my friend Alain, he is waiting for me all this time. So I went with him.' The old boyfriend came back looking for her. It had not worked with the American. But she had just gotten married. 'Then he married, too. I got divorced. He is divorcing now. This man, it's Laurent. He will move in here in a few months.' She counts on her fingers. 'Twenty-one years late. What I am saying, these decisions we make in youth are everything. You have no idea. Those feelings, they don't revenir. Pas comme ça. And no one tells you.' She points to the pages of Yash's letter on the bed. 'Do not put this love second. Marry him. Marry him and have your babies. It doesn't matter what happens after that.' I say I'm only twenty-three and she says, 'Screw the calendar. What does a calendar know about love?'

## HEART THE LOVER

\* \* \*

'Let him go,' my friend Nobiko, who takes care of the twins on the fourth floor, says to me. She is divorced. She hung on too long. Trop longtemps, she says. It's June. I'm waiting for a letter again. The next day a letter comes and I show it to her. She says something in Japanese then translates it into French. Something about a petit poisson. He's keeping you on the hook, is what she means.

I find some cheap French classes and make a few friends in them. I bring the kids, Luc and Delphine, to their lessons and playdates all over the city. I try to study grammar. I try to read. In my tiny room I start to write a couple of short stories but don't finish them. Most of my writing comes out in the form of letters to Yash, in which I try to stay upbeat and anecdotal and not overwhelm him with my longing for him, and the journal I keep for the overspill of that emotion. I am so in love with him it is hard to take a full breath, I write in the journal. His absence feels like losing a lung.

My life is pending, suspended. It swings from letter to letter. When one arrives, I soar for a week straight. Over the next week, I come down slowly. Once back on the ground I fear the worst. He's met someone, someone who makes him feel different, new, even more alive. She is Brazilian. She is a dancer. She is a Brazilian dancer and I will never hear from him again. Then a fresh letter arrives and up I go again.

His first packet from Knoxville in June is exuberant. He's graduated with highest honors, he's set up a table and chair in his father's barn, and he's made a vow to start a novel, five pages a day. This makes me so happy I don't force myself to wait a few days. I write back immediately. I have so much I want to say, I tell him, that everything is bubbling up fast and jamming together. 'And still,' I write, 'there is this sense that I could express it all in just one nonexistent word and you would understand exactly what I mean.'

His July letter is shorter and less buoyant. His father is a despot at work, his mother is chaos incarnate. He would leave town tomorrow but he has to save for France. He is reading Kafka, he says, 'possibly not the best choice for the moment in question.' At the end of the letter he tells me he wrote nine of the worst pages of fiction ever committed to paper and they have been befittingly burned with the brush pile behind the tool shed.

And finally he is here. I go to Charles de Gaulle to meet him and bring him back to my little bed. The family, like most Parisians in August, has left the city. They've gone to Léa's mother's in Saint-Malo. We have the apartment to ourselves. We lie down on our sides facing each other, the only way we can fit on the narrow mattress, pressed as close as we can be. He is new but familiar, precious, thrilling. 'I think it's safe to say I love you,' he says. We move slowly—he's been awake for over twenty-four hours—and have slow tiny-bed sex. He comes and calls me babe when we are sweaty and spent. 'I didn't know how much I missed you,' he says.

Our first week together we stay in Paris. I take him to all the places where I ached for him. It was like bringing him home to kindly relatives who would share my joy. Here he is, I say to the horse chestnuts in the Luco, to my booth at Le Danton, and to the spot on the grass in the Champs de Mars where I read his most recent letter. Here he is.

We make our own Proust tour and see his recreated bedroom at the Carnavalet, with pieces of the cork he used to line his bedroom walls. We go to 102 Haussmann, now a bank, where he lived for thirteen years while writing *La Recherche* and where, Dr. Gastrell told us, in September of 1914 he sobbed in the moonlight when a German invasion of the city seemed imminent. We find the alley down which Swann went to find Odette's bedroom door.

We go out one night with my friends from French class, Irish Deirdre and Dutch Loes and Loes' friend Fabien from Toulouse. We meet at a basement bar near the Pantheon and squeeze into a table in the corner. I go to get us drinks and look back at him there with my new friends, elbows on the table, head tipped to the side, his rooster cowlick, his mischievous grin. He's telling them a story. I have that familiar impatience to get back to the table so I don't miss what he's saying.

Madame Trèves made me promise I would go to her favorite restaurant, Lapis, and I'd waited to go with Yash, but once he sees the menu on its little stand outside the blue-and-gold door, he won't splurge on the prix fixe meal. He worked all summer to afford this trip, but he doesn't seem to want to spend any of the money he saved.

I take him to an inexpensive Indian restaurant in the 5th that I like, Le Punjab. I'd never had Indian food until I moved to Paris. We walk in and a woman in back calls out to us and Yash answers and I don't know what either of them has said. He always claimed he spoke no Hindi. She shows us the only table in the window, raised up on a platform so you have to step up onto it, and her husband brings over the menus. The couple chat with Yash and I can tell he is telling them that he doesn't speak much, but they disagree and tell me in French that he speaks very well.

Where in India is his family from, they want to know and instead of saying Delhi Yash says something else and they don't know it so they get out a map and they all look at it together and can't find the town. They ask him a question in Hindi he doesn't understand and they ask it to me.

'Comment s'écrit ce village?'

'Je ne suis pas sûr,' Yash says and they are thrilled he understands French, too.

They bring the woman's father out from the back and go through it again and the old man doesn't know the town either.

We never order. They just start bringing out dishes. They fuss over us. They think Yash is marvelous.

On the way home he says, 'They were such kind people, weren't they?'

'They were.'

He is silent for a long time. I take his hand. We're walking up Mouffetard. We have it all to ourselves. The shops are closed, the restaurants quiet. The Parisians are gone and the tourists aren't interested in this part of town at night.

'That is the first time I've ever been to an Indian restaurant.'

'You don't have any in Knoxville?'

'We have one. I could never go there. I was raised with India as the Death Star. You couldn't mention it. My second-grade teacher gave me an extra credit assignment on India and my father tried to get her fired.'

He lets go of my hand and rubs his face and is quiet again. Then he says, 'Four years of college and I never studied its history or Hindi. I've never read an Indian writer. Let's go there. I'm not sure my father would ever speak to me again but let's go. Will you come? Someday?'

'Of course.'

In bed that night he tells me he has only one recurring dream, that he is giving his father's eulogy. 'It's an embarrassing cliché. I'm standing there, sometimes in a church, sometimes in a field, once inside a storage unit—but it's always good, my eulogy. It feels sort of the same from dream to dream. Off the cuff, no notes. But it feels like I've said it before. It's a very good speech. People love it. My mother and my stepmother are right up front and they are weeping and holding hands. I nail it, every time.'

'And your father is never there to hear it.'

'Nope. He's always dead.'

I convince him that we, too, need to get out of the city. We take a train to Strasbourg and another to Davos. Yash wants to see the sanatorium where Thomas Mann visited his wife, Katia, for three weeks in 1912, the visit that inspired *The Magic Mountain*. The air is as clean and sharp as it is in all the books when tubercular characters go seeking a cure. We feel lightheaded, walking up to our inn from the train station, the Alps rising on all sides, the highest peaks pale blue with ice. Later we stand in front of the enormous building, still a sanatorium, for asthma now that tuberculosis can be cured. It looks like a giant hotel with big balconies off every room where the patients would spend their days breathing in the cold, clear air. We walk around the grounds and imagine we are consumptive strangers meeting there, like Hans Castorp and Clawdia Chauchat. Chauchat, he tells me, was the name of the machine gun used by the French in World War I.

The next morning we go for a day hike, twelve kilometers to a southern peak. We start early in order to get down by dark. The innkeeper's son packs us a lunch and snacks. He is our age, blond and broad, a bit mechanical when he speaks English. Yash is convinced he has a thing for me, and he has this running joke on the hike that the Swiss man is behind a tree or a boulder.

On the trail we talk as we often do about books, what makes the magic, where the genius lies. He says it's in the structure. It's always in the structure. We argue about this. I insist it can be in a number of elements—the images, the dialogue, all the ways in which the narrative comes to life—and he says it's always the form that makes the difference. I say the structure of *War and Peace* was no great shakes, and he breaks the book down for me section by section to show how Tolstoy was reconceiving both *The Iliad* and *The Aeneid* to build his masterpiece.

The trail is narrow, the trees tall on either side. An occasional footbridge stretches over a stream. During the first hour we have glimpses of the town below getting smaller through the trees. The next hour or so we have no views, then with no warning the sky opens up and the land flattens into a meadow flush with pink and red flowers.

'I warned you this might happen.'

'You did,' he says.

I put down my backpack and run through the grass with my arms stretched out. I spin around and around and begin to sing that the hills are alive as loudly as possible. Eventually I peter out and Yash joins me in the grass near the lip of the ridge and we lie there and feel the mountains and their shadows and we take off our clothes and have sex until three cows come trotting quickly toward us in an aggressive, uncowlike way, each with a big loud bell around its neck, and we leap up naked and laughing and unsure of which way to go. They abruptly change direction and we lie down in the grass again and their clanging fades away slowly.

Yash traces his fingers over my neck and shoulders. 'I think for the rest of my life the sound of cowbells will make me horny.'

Closer to the peak we come to a dark green pool surrounded by flat rocks. We take off our clothes again. The water is very cold. Not long ago it was ice. I want to play in the water together, ride on his back, kiss in his arms, everything slick and sexy. But he swims away from me across to the other side. I get out and stand on a warm rock, the cool water dripping from my hair down my back and legs into a pool at my feet. The sun dries my skin. It feels polished and alive. He comes out of the water and stands beside me. He takes my hand and I feel relieved. I press my lips to his neck and hold him close and more water from his hair drips down my back and shoulders and my skin tightens as it evaporates. I tell him I love him with my whole heart.

    I look up at him and his mouth is twisted.

    'What's the matter?'

    He doesn't answer.

    'You okay, Hink?'

    He shakes his head. 'It just hurts a little, to feel this good.'

When we come back to Paris at the end of August, Léa and her children are home. Yash and I take them to tennis lessons on the Métro and shop for food and make them meals. The kids grow attached to him quickly and Léa tells me that if he weren't so marvelous she would never let him stay in my room. Yash and Laurent argue volubly about topics as disparate as NATO and prosecco. A week before Yash is supposed to fly home, Laurent offers him a job at his company in something called *l'intelligence artificielle*, which I've never heard of before and will for a long time think of as exclusively French. Laurent insists it is an exciting and promising field. He has a friend in the Ministry of the Interior who can move the papers quickly. Yash thinks about it for a few days and accepts. He's going to stay! He will make a real salary. We can get an apartment and I'll finish out the year working for Lèa, then I can teach private English classes and really start to write.

On the night before he was supposed to fly back, he goes to the phone booth around the corner to ask his dad to send over some clothes and books. And there in that glass box, in less than ten minutes, he has a change of heart.

At first I think I can change it back. 'This is a rare opportunity,' I say. 'Laurent is going to get you a *work permit*. Mr. Cautious needs to carpe diem a little.'

'Or it could be a year of French bureaucracy and getting deported before the paperwork comes through.' His father has gotten to him so fast.

'What does your dad think is a better idea for you?'

'It's not him. I'd been thinking maybe I should stick to my original plan.'

Original plan? I have not heard of this plan.

'To save enough to move to New York.'

New York?

'A guy I know from high school is there. He's working at Houghton Mifflin. Entry-level position, though he's pretty plugged-in already. He had dinner with Philip Roth last month.'

I've never been to New York. It always looks so bleak in movies. This plan makes no sense to me.

'Paris is better in every way than New York.'

'Not for being a writer.'

'Yeah. Think of all the crappy novels that have been written here. *Ulysses, The Sun Also Rises, Madame Bovary.*' I have no idea where *Madame Bovary* was written and hope he doesn't either.

'New York is the hub that Paris used to be,' he says.

We stay up all night, his last night, going around and around on this. Didn't we spend last fall dreaming of living in Paris? What happened to that? What happened?

'So,' he says, softening, nuzzling up to me, 'you don't want to live in New York?'

'Not really.'

'With me.'

'I like trees.'

'With me, near a park?'

'When?'

'When I save up.'

It feels like such a mistake, him going back and working for his father again, miserable, when he could be here and we could be together right now.

Our last sex is sad. Or at least it is for me.

The first pale light comes through the window. In an hour he'll have to go to the airport. I can't stop crying.

'How about January?' he says. 'I can make enough by January.'

He leaves. Paris loses all its luster without him. There is a bare space in my room where his green duffel used to be. I am the facteur again, checking the silver box morning and night. He barely writes. He says he is working as many hours as his dad will pay him for, sometimes sixty hours a week. I take on tutoring jobs while the kids are at school. I stop going out. I buy nothing. I save for New York.

By the middle of October, I need to hear his voice. I go to the pay phone at the corner on a Sunday afternoon. As it rings I pray Yash or his stepmother will answer, but I am not lucky.

His father acts like my name is only vaguely familiar to him. I ask him if he could ask Yash to please call me when he gets a chance.

'Does he have your number?'

'Yes.'

'Are you still in Europe?'

'Yes.'

'That will be an expensive phone call. Which will appear on my bill.'

'I'm sure he'll reimburse you.'

'Wouldn't your words be prettier in a letter?'

The pay phone beeps. I have ten seconds to put in another coin or be cut off.

'I'll do that. Thank you, Mr. Thakkar.'

Yash does not call back.

I write Carson in Brooklyn about rentals, and she writes back fast saying a friend of a friend was looking to sublet her prewar walk-up between the Navy Yard and the bridge. I don't know what any of it means. I send Yash the friend's address and phone number and tell Carson we're interested.

A few weeks later one of Yash's packets comes, the yellow legal sheets of paper full of complaints about his father and whiskey distribution and the cubical he shares with a man who smells like mayonnaise and vapor rub. On the last page he says he talked to Carson's friend and the place sounded decent. He would send her a check at the end of the week and she would send him the keys. We could move in on January 1.

To save money I don't fly home for the holidays. Léa and Laurent go to Rome, and her children spend the vacation with their father in the 16th. I have a few students who stay in the city, and I squeeze out a few more francs from them before I go.

Yash calls me on Christmas Day. He wants to know if I'm okay. He hasn't heard from me in a while.

'The shoe is on the other foot.' I can hear how strange my voice sounds.

'What's wrong, Hink?'

'I'm tired. I'm tired of missing you.'

Words feel useless. I just need to see him.

'I get it,' he says. 'It's been a long fall.'

'It has.'

We talk about the logistics of early January. He says his flight to Newark lands an hour after mine, giving me time to get through customs. We're both flying Delta. We'll meet at baggage claim. He received the keys to the apartment. He promises he won't forget them.

I get to baggage claim fifteen minutes before his flight lands. I lean on my big suitcase, an old oatmeal-colored one of my mother's, and wait for his flight to appear on the screen. Finally it does. Carousel 3. I drag my oatmeal bag over there and sit again. It is moving but there are no bags on it yet. Two women come down the escalator and stand close to the conveyor belt. I go over to them and ask if they've come from Knoxville. They have. Yash has landed. I go back to my perch on the suitcase.

'Someone's happy,' a man with a Delta badge says to me as he walks by.

I watch the escalator. The backs of my legs prickle. My gut aches. My stomach has been upset all week. I think of sharing a bathroom with him again. Hinky Stinky, he used to say. All the people coming down the escalator now and standing at Carousel 3 waiting for their bags to appear on the conveyor belt are precious to me because they've been on a flight with Yash. I know he'll be one of the last off. He walks slowly. He'll stop in the bathroom, sip from the cooler. 'He sounds a bit low energy if you ask me,' my mother said once on the phone. This surprised me. What did I say to give her that impression? His mind works so quickly. Low energy? I watch more people glide diagonally down. None of them with his sweet face.

If he knew how much I loved him it would terrify him. I think of Willie in sixth grade, asking me out by the swing set. He called me every night that week. We talked a lot about his hamsters, Sailor and Glory. Glory stuffed her cheeks with seeds and you could press her neck and feel them all in there like a bean bag chair, he told me. Sailor didn't do that. Willie and I met at the mall that Saturday, walked around holding hands. Before our parents came to pick us up, he kissed me outside the bathrooms by the food court. He said I was a good kisser and I told him about my crush on him since the beginning of third grade. I told him I remembered a pale blue shirt he used to wear that year, and the little drawings of rabbits he used to make at the back of his math workbook in fourth grade. He called the next day and broke up with me. Why, I asked before my throat closed and the tears started. He said it was too much pressure. All that stuff I'd said about liking him for so long. He said it made him feel like Sailor.

'Why?' I whispered.

'Because you have all these memories of me stuffed inside you and I don't, and it makes me feel funny.'

I sit on my suitcase thinking about that phone conversation. It was kind of a great comparison. And he was so honest. I haven't told Yash that story. I didn't want him to see it as a cautionary tale. When we're in our walk-up I'll tell him about Willie Sylvester. He'll like that name. Good name for a character, he'll say.

Suitcases start emerging from a hole in the middle of the carousel, up and over they go, sliding down to the belt. It happens fast, the way people grab them and disappear. Soon there is only one silver suitcase going around and around. It isn't his. I go to look at the arrival board. There's another flight from Knoxville in two hours. I go to the bathroom. I pass a bank of pay phones but I don't use one. I wait. After an hour, I go to the phones and call Carson to see if Yash has left a message for me. He hasn't. The next flight from Knoxville lands and Yash is not on that either.

I go back to the phones and dial his dad's number. My heart is pounding.

I'm trying not to cry but I'm crying. His stepmother answers. A small blessing.

'Oh, Jordan, we worried it would be you.'

'What happened?' I hear my voice ring against the three walls of phones.

'Oh, sweetie. Calm yourself. He's fine. He told me to tell you he'd be on the road till late and that he'd give you a call at Carson's tomorrow.'

'On the road? He's *driving* here?'

She doesn't answer.

'He's bringing his car to New York?' He decided against that months ago.

'He's not driving to New York, hon. He's gone to Atlanta. To Sam's.'

Somehow I find a cab to Brooklyn. I howl the whole way. The driver never says a word. It's New York. He's seen it all.

I press her buzzer and Carson comes down in her old slippers.

My coat can't button anymore so she sees the shape of me, the mess I've made.

'Oh, honey.'

I wail in her arms.

'Does he know?'

I shake my head.

'Oh, my little chicken,' she says.

She holds me for a long time, then she carries my heavy suitcase up the stairs.

II

My boys unleash themselves from the back, shove open their doors, and race across the dirt road to the silver slide. Their steps ring out on its metal rungs.

'That's old school,' you say about the slide as we trail behind them.

Why are you here, is what I want to say.

The park is on a long finger of land that pokes into the Atlantic. The water glints and dances through the pines all around us.

Harry gets to the top first, Jack right behind him, grabbing onto his brother's back. They drop down fast. Jack tumbles sideways off into the dirt and pulls Harry with him and they're rolling and laughing. They're five and seven, my boys.

You watch, shake your head. 'That thing is way too high and way too steep. Are there no safety codes up here?'

'I'll have to check the paperwork on that, Mr. Cautious.'

You look at me and laugh. The boys get up from the ground and run back to climb up again. Jack makes it to the steps first.

I wait for you to say the things people like to say about Jack, about his speed, his fearlessness, how he'd soon be giving his older brother a run for his money.

'They're happy kids,' you say as they slide down again.

'You've been here less than two hours.'

'I can tell. All my friends' kids are fucked up. These ones seem okay.'

You bend down and pick up a brown pine needle off the ground. 'God, when was the last time I saw one of these?'

As if I know.

'Harry! Jack!' You jog toward them. You had a runner's body once, sharp glutes beneath the band of your gray sweats. Now it looks like things hurt. 'Let's climb one of these.' You're pointing to the pine trees behind the swings, silhouettes against the dark, sparkling ocean.

I don't think Jack has climbed a tree yet. They look at me and I nod and they run to you. They each take a hand. Does this surprise you? Jack starts to skip. How easy they both are with you. They normally hold back with other men, men who aren't their father.

You choose a tree. I'm stationed at its base. Up you all go. I have to lift Jack up to get his feet on the first branch and then he climbs like a spider monkey.

'Higher?' you say to them.

'Higher!' my boys chime.

There are creaks and snaps of tiny twigs and then you stop before I have to say anything and the boys climb up to where you are and stop, too.

'Mumma, can you still see us?' Jack says. He's straddling a big limb, patting it like a horse. If he slips, I can easily catch him.

'Barely,' I say.

Your three faces are looking down on me, the bottoms of your sneakers swinging. You tell them the story about Daphne fleeing from Apollo through the woods, running, running, calling to her father the river god for help, then her arms becoming branches and her feet roots. You put your hand flat on the tree's trunk. 'And for a few seconds,' you tell them, 'Apollo can feel her heartbeat through the bark.'

The boys press their hands to the trunk, too.

A squirrel leaps from the tree next door onto a high branch, looks down, and leaps back in surprise. The three of you laugh and the tree's needles tremble.

What do you know and why are you here?

You and the boys come down the tree.

'My highest is eleven,' Harry is saying.

'What? That's crazytown,' you say.

'Mine is nine and a half,' Jack says.

'A half?' you say. 'I want to see a half.'

Then you are all too far away to hear, sprinting toward the water, leaping down the little embankment of scrub grass. When you reach the wet sand the three of you slow down and start taking stooped steps, looking for flat stones.

A disheveled dog, barely bigger than a squirrel and a lot faster, starts running circles around me and yapping.

'Fabio!'

An older woman comes across the playground with a thin leash. 'I'm sorry. He slipped by me when I opened the car door.'

Fabio stops moving when she bends to clip on the leash. He even extends his tiny neck for her.

'Cute dog,' I say.

She straightens up and looks toward the water. 'Cute kids.'

We watch the boys on the beach, their thick hair and wiry bodies. They're showing you their rock-skimming technique, arcing back on one foot, bending low, and releasing a flat stone across the surface just the way Silas taught them. Jack jumps up and down on the sand. Harry cranks his arm around over his head. You give it a try and up comes a great holler of surprise. You bend down low for their high fives.

'Cute dad, too,' the woman says.

'He's not their dad.' I regret how sharply I say this.

She isn't bothered. 'You sure?'

I laugh. The three dark heads on the beach search for more flat stones. 'First time I've seen him in years.' Twenty-one years.

'Ah.'

'Yeah.'

I love how fast women get things.

Another cheer from the beach. Jack takes a victory lap then waves for me to come. I give Fabio a little scrub between the ears and head to the water.

In the car on the way home the boys are sleepy. You tell me about a book you read over the winter, a novel about Iceland and sheep. Silas has parked behind your rental in our driveway, so I park on the street. Jack's friend Otis sticks his head into the open passenger window.

'Crater time,' he says. Then he notices you an inch from his face. 'Who's this?'

He doesn't wait for an answer. He hustles Harry and Jack out of the car and they all run to his yard next door.

'Crater?' you say.

'It's a game they made up. I think it takes place on the moon.'

On our way to the house, you stop at your rental and pull your bag out of the back. It's the green duffel you brought to Paris. Now it's come to Maine. The sight of it is jarring. I wish you would put it back in the car. I wish I hadn't offered you a place to stay on your trip up the coast to see friends.

Silas and I moved up here from Massachusetts before Harry was born. We sold our tiny apartment in Cambridge for more than the price of this three-bedroom in Portland. It's an old house, low ceilings, horsehair poking out of the plaster, the remnants of a wooden latrine in the downstairs closet.

You follow me up onto the side porch and through the door. Our dogs skitter loudly across the pine floor of the kitchen to smell you. You squat to give them your full attention.

'Who's this?' you say, mimicking Otis perfectly to our bulldog Nelson, who mashes her face into yours. 'And who's this?' you say to Maxie the beagle while his hard tail thwaps loudly against the rungs of a chair. You look up at me. 'I didn't know you had dogs.'

I shrug. Why would you?

On cue, Lupe, who was in a crouch beneath the wood stove, struts across the kitchen and presses her forehead to your knee. 'Or a woeful cat.' You stroke her from tip to tail. 'Your characters never have pets.'

I don't know what of mine you've read.

I take your bag and put it by the stairs.

'Wow,' you say, looking left into the living room. 'It's like walking into the Breach House.'

'Why?'

'It just feels like it.'

I get two beers from the fridge and get you back outside. Our house is nothing like the Breach. We sit in the two beat-up wicker chairs on our porch. You answer my questions about your work and I answer yours about mine. I barely know what I'm saying. It's so strange you're here, and so unnerving how familiar you are, the rhythm of your voice, the tilt of your head, the shifts of your body, the hair on your wrists, the scar on your lip. Every now and then I can hear my boys next door and their voices keep some part of me rooted. And some part of me is aware that Silas is home and hasn't come down. The house is too small for him not to know we're back. I wonder where he is and if it's odd that I haven't gone to find him and if that seems strange to you.

You tell me about a case you worked on for two years, a slam-dunk corruption suit against a school for the deaf that was extorting its students, only to have it be dismissed due to sexual misconduct by your assistant attorney. 'He was sleeping with the head of the school,' you say. 'He's still sleeping with her. I went to their wedding last month.'

I laugh and shut my eyes and wish I could keep them shut. The familiarity is too much. It goes too deep. I don't know why you've come. And I can't hear the boys anymore. Where is Silas?

\* \* \*

I stayed in Brooklyn with Carson for a week. My oatmeal suitcase took up a quarter of her studio. When the phone rang while she was at work, I didn't answer it. When she was home, I refused to speak to you. Carson told me you told her bullshit things about savings and timing, about how your friend in publishing had left for a job in finance, how you could write a draft of a novel on the cheap in Atlanta, which was much more affordable than New York. You tried out a Homeric allusion to the thread of fate.

'Are you in or out?' Carson asked.

You didn't answer.

'Then let her go,' she said, and put down the phone.

I went to my mother's in Phoenix. I was there five months. Strange to say, under the circumstances, but it was a beautiful time with her. My last long uninterrupted time with her before she died. She did not once question my decisions. I needed help and she gave it to me without hesitation. She found the agency and sat with me on their loveseat as we looked through three-ring binders of people without names or addresses, just professions, personal statements, and photographs. I chose the couple looking at each other, not at the camera. She did the classes with me. I didn't want the drugs. When I went into labor, the only place I could look was in her eyes. 'You are going to be okay,' she said to me, over and over. When the baby finally came, it was my mother who said, 'Oh sweetie, it's a girl.' We had an hour with her, then a proper goodbye. She was never mine. I always knew that. I could not keep her.

In my head I call her Daisy.

Sometimes she comes to me, more a feeling than a vision, a warmth, not a regret. I worry about many things, but I never worry about Daisy. Somehow I know she is well.

We sit on the porch with our beers.

'You have a real life here, don't you?'

'I do. I imagine you have a real life, too.'

'I don't.' You look down and rub your jeans. It makes me remember this cassette tape I had of Faulkner reading *As I Lay Dying*. We listened to it in your car a lot. *Anse keeps on rubbing his knees.* That was our favorite line. The Deep South cadence created a strong drumbeat. *Anse keeps on rubbing his knees.* We repeated it randomly for months. For a moment I think you're going to say it, and maybe you are, but Silas comes up the driveway.

He's been on a run. He often runs after work. Somehow I'd forgotten this.

He's flushed and a little sweaty. He comes up the steps two at a time and normally we'd do some hugging and kissing and he'd try to mush me against his damp

T-shirt and I'd pretend to be grossed out, but now we are self-conscious in front of you. I go for a kiss and he a hug, and my jaw hits his ear.

The two of you shake hands. You sit back down and Silas leans against the railing and asks about your drive up from Logan, and who you're going to see up the coast.

I say I have to start dinner, and flee.

I was in grad school in Pennsylvania three years later when the phone rang late one night. 'Ivan died,' you said.

He had died that morning. It was impossible to hang up. I listened. Ivan had gotten an infection that tore through his intestines in a few weeks. You and Sam had been there in the hospital with him the whole time. At the end you took turns reading him Joyce. Shakespeare. Dylan Thomas.

We talked for three hours. At some point you started reading me some of those passages that you'd read to Ivan. Then you read something that made you think of me, you said. It was from *Journey to the End of the Night* by Céline. The narrator was remembering a goodbye he'd had with a girl named Molly at a train station. He hadn't said goodbye properly, he hadn't appreciated what they'd had together. It was beautiful. Full of regret. There was a line about how he'd kissed her but not as he should have. I've tried to find that passage in that book so many times but I never have.

You read me those lines, but you didn't say more about them, and I didn't ask you to. We did not speak of what blew us apart. I did not tell you about our child or that I could not write a story in grad school without a baby in it.

You called a few more times that winter. You asked if we could see each other in the spring and I said no. Oh, how I wanted to see you, that lonely winter in Pennsylvania. Those calls reawakened all the love and all the wounds. I couldn't trust you again with my heart. I was glad when you didn't call back.

The next year I got a poem in the mail. A poem by D. H. Lawrence copied out in blue ballpoint on yellow legal paper.

'The elephant, the huge old beast,' it began, 'is slow to mate.' They wait 'for the sympathy in their vast shy hearts slowly, slowly to rouse.'

I wasn't an elephant. My heart had never been slow. I tore it up.

You and Silas stay on the porch. I'm glad to have the kitchen to myself, glad for a break from your unsound observations. The Breach was fussy, grandmotherly, frozen in 1957. Our house full of children and animals is nothing like that. Silas is laughing. He'll be indifferent to your scrutiny of him. He might notice it, but he won't take interest in the verdict. Once, as we were leaving the house after dinner with a couple we didn't know well, we heard one of them say through an open window, 'Well, what'd you think of that?' I slowed to hear the response, and Silas tugged me down the driveway. He did not want to know.

Your conversation sounds animated, from what reaches me through the screen door. I season the chicken legs and put them in under the broiler. I trim the asparagus, drop them into the steamer. I see you come in and go through the living room to the bathroom. On your way out you stop in the doorway and ask if I need help. I send you back to the porch with another beer. Setting the table, I can hear you two talking about *The Invisible Man*. You must have asked Silas what he was teaching in the fall. I call to Silas to round up the boys from next door and you both go across the yard. You come back all together ten minutes later, Harry and Jack explaining the rules of Crater to you.

'But why can't you go in and get the three rocks and win right at the start?' you say.

'Because only one side knows where the crater is.'

Your eyes widen. 'The crater changes locations?'

'Yes!'

'And size?'

'Yes!'

'Genius,' you say.

We sit at the table, you between the boys. Jack's feet knock against his chair in excitement. He likes you.

'Look at this feast,' you say. 'Do you get this every night?'

'Yup,' Harry says.

I had enough time while everyone was across the street to make some hollandaise.

Jack passes you the little bowl of it. 'You have to try this. It's really excellent.'

You smile at me for this praise. You know my sauces—I learned them all in Paris. Without testing it, you pour the hollandaise over everything and that makes them all laugh. You start cutting up your chicken and I know exactly how you'll eat it, fork in your left hand, chicken, asparagus, and hollandaise all piled up on the back of it.

For a few minutes there's only the scrape and clash of silverware on dinner plates. They all eat like jackals, not just you.

'Why is there a photograph of Crested Butte in the bathroom?' you ask. 'Are you from there?'

Silas smiles and shakes his head.

'Papa asked her on a date,' Harry says, 'but he drove to Crested Butte instead.'

'Really?'

'Then he sent her that postcard and she forgave him.'

'All it took was a postcard?'

'Yeah, and it's mostly about a dog he saw in a store.'

'Wow.'

'Are you married?' Jack asks.

'No sir, I am not,' you say.

'Do you have a significant other?' Harry asks, a term he's just learned.

'Not at this moment.' You take another bite. 'But do you know what happened to me on a date once?'

The boys shake their heads eagerly.

I can't imagine what he's about to tell them about a date.

'Well. I went out with this perfectly nice lady. We had a very nice dinner, at the end of which I asked if she would like to visit the bookstore across the street— a large chain, not the kind of cozy bookshop you have in these parts. She was amenable and off we went. And right there as we entered the store was a display table with piles and piles of one book and beside these piles was a life-size poster of . . . Guess who?' After a few seconds you tip your head my way.

'Mumma?' Harry says.

'This is not a true story,' I say.

'It *is* a true story. You'd just won that prize. And my date says, "Oh, I *loved* that book."'

'Maybe there was a little photocopied flyer.'

'Life-size poster.'

'Did you tell her?' Jack said.

'That I knew your mother? No. I was speechless.'

'Did you go out with her again?'

'Never saw her after that night.'
'Do you have a job?' Harry asks.
'Yes.'
'What is it?'
'It's very, very boring.'
They think this is very funny.
'But what do you do?'
'I litigate.'
'What's that?'
'I spend months and years sometimes trying to prove in a court of law that one plus one equals two, and most of the time at the end of it all a judge will say, no, I'm sorry, one plus one equals three and a half.'
'Why?'
'It's just the way the law works.'
'We're about to lose one of our best teachers to law school,' Silas says. 'Maybe you could come convince her that her lousy salary is actually a blessing in disguise?'
'Gladly. Though law school was a blast. It's what comes after it that's unpleasant.'

When we're finished, the boys clear the dishes and Silas gets out ice cream and a strawberry rhubarb pie he must have bought with the asparagus. The boys are surprised by the dessert. I smile at Silas. It's a sweet, special-occasion gesture.

Harry eats his quickly. He likes to draw after dinner. It's part of our ritual. Then Jack will choose a game.

You watch him across the table. 'Clearly Harry's going to be an artist.' You turn to Jack. 'What about you, peanut?'

'Olympic athlete.'

'Which event?'

'I haven't narrowed that down yet.'

You laugh at how he says this. 'Well, you still have some time.'

I watch Harry draw a tree. Somehow he knows about shading. He's filling in the trunk now, making shadows. I bend closer. He's drawn a face just below where the branches split.

'What's her name?' he asks without looking up.

'Daphne,' I say.

Jack leans over you to see the drawing. 'That is so cool.'

Harry tears it out of his sketchbook and hands it to you. 'You can have it if you want.'

'Really?' You look down at the drawing. I see your old face briefly, when it was more expressive, full of feeling. Your new face is guarded, slower to react. 'Thank you.'

It is perhaps as confusing for you to be here as it is for me.

Jack takes our bowls to the sink and puts a deck of cards on the table. 'What are we playing?'

'Do you mind?' I say to you.

'No. Cards are great,' you say. I can tell you haven't played a card game in a long time.

Jack shuffles and you laugh as his small hands split, riffle, and bridge the deck back together. 'Only a child of yours could do that so young,' you say.

We've been in a Rummy 500 phase all summer so it's a surprise when Jack says, 'Sir Hincomb Funnibuster?'

'No,' Harry says. 'It takes too long to teach.'

'You can make a chart,' Jack says.

'I know how to play,' you say.

The boys don't believe you. No one outside our family has ever heard of this game. You insist that you do, and they tell you to prove it by naming a whole family.

You smile. You love a challenge to your memory. 'All right.' You look at Silas. 'Sir Hincomb Funnibuster.'

The boys nod.

You look at me. 'Sir Hincomb Funnibuster's wife.' You nodded at Harry. 'Sir Hincomb Funnibuster's eldest son.' You turn to Jack. 'Sir Hincomb Funnibuster's ten children.' You glance over at the dogs, asleep on the couches beyond the wood stove. 'Sir Hincomb Funnibuster's nine servants.' The boys laugh. You pause. You look around for the cat but she's vanished. 'Sir Hincomb Funnibuster's parrot.'

'No!' The boys shake their heads furiously.

'You always forget the donkey,' I say.

You grin at me. 'I do. I always forget the donkey.' I can't help smiling back. 'Okay. The donkey, the parrot, the twins, and the baby!'

'How does he know?' Harry asks me.

'Our friend Ivan taught it to us. Many years ago.'

'I didn't know it came from Ivan,' Silas says.

Harry can't understand this, these years before him, before our family existed. He looks at Silas. 'You weren't there?'

Silas shakes his head. 'I didn't know them then.'

Jack, dealing out the cards, is taking in this information easily, but Harry looks like he would like to go up to his room and mull over questions of time and existence for a few hours.

We fan out our cards. Silas keeps his low, close to the table. He's started to do that lately, hold things farther away to read them. You're making the little humming noises you always make when organizing your hand.

'You're left of the dealer,' Jack tells you.

'Oh, excuse me. Silas?' I could tell you were up to a little mischief.

'Yes.'

'May I please have Heart the Lover?'

'Yes, you may.' Silas passes the king of hearts face up, close to you, trying to get you to touch it before saying thank you.

'I thought you might,' you say and reach for the card and we get ready to scream. A half inch before you touch it you say, 'Thank you,' and pick up the king with a flourish that makes the boys laugh. 'Silas,' you continue.

'Yes.'

'May I please have Heart the Lover's wife?'

'No, you may not.'

'Well, you can't blame a guy for trying,' he says.

Silas and I chuckle and Harry asks why that was funny and now I'm the one who wants to go upstairs to ponder time and existence for a while.

I lose twice. I don't keep track of what people have. Jack is dismayed by my poor performance. He and Harry, flushed and hoarse from the yelling, beg for another round, but Silas tells them to say their goodnights. They stand up reluctantly. I hug them tight and kiss their steamy hair. You stand up and say you'll be off early in the morning and might not see them and they both wrap their arms around your waist. Silas says he might miss you, too, as he has to be at school at seven tomorrow.

'Great meeting you after all this time,' Silas says and gives you a loose hug and a few pats.

I don't want them to go upstairs but they do.

'Good guy,' you say.

'Yeah. He is.' I go to put the kettle on. 'Tea?'

'Sure.'

You lean your back against the kitchen counter as we wait for the water to boil. I feel a bit giddy from the game and terrified to be alone with you.

'Does he maybe look a little like Sam?'

'Seriously?'

'In the face? Around the mouth maybe?' You push your lips together with your fingers.

'No. Stop.'

My alarm amuses you.

'Good lord.' I get mugs from the shelf, boxes of tea from the cabinet. I need to redirect things. 'So, are you seeing anyone?'

'Like a shrink?'

'Like a person.'

'No shrink. No woman. No cry.' You smile at your little joke.

On one of our first dates Silas told me when he was younger he thought it was 'No Woman, No Crime.'

'No dating?'

'I participate in the courting ritual from time to time.' You choose a teabag and a mug. 'It's scary out there, now that I have this profession. Women like a guy with a job. They love a worker bee. It's like they see the pollen on my legs.' He brushes his pants with both hands. 'But what else am I going to do with my time? All my friends have disappeared into their houses. I only see them if I get invited to the sidelines of one of their kids' soccer games. What is it with soccer? It's so fucked up.'

I tap the photo of Jack's peewee team on the fridge.

'Et tu, Brute?' you say.

We take our teas to the couches in the family room. You sit on one and I sit on the other. The dogs follow us in and jump up beside you. You look to the wall of bookshelves Silas and the boys built earlier in the summer.

'I didn't picture you living in a house.'

'I know. It's weird.'

'After all those tiny rooms. Your room on Pye Street?'

All bed, you once said.

'And that little closet in Paris?'

'Chambre de bonne,' I say.

'Chambre de merde, didn't we call it?'

'Something like that.'

'I can't believe you don't see the similarities to the Breach. That radiator.' You point to our big black radiator in the corner. 'We had the same one. Remember? In the hallway across from the bathroom.'

'It's a radiator.'

'And the moldings on your doorways, with the circles at the top corners? Same.'

I don't remember the moldings.

'It's uncanny.'

I picture you going back to Atlanta and telling this to Sam. *It's uncanny. She's re-created the Breach in Maine right down to the moldings.*

'I haven't lived in a house since then,' you say.

'You have. MacDougal Street.'

'That was just a room. It didn't feel like a house.'

'You should rent one, then. Or buy one. Worker bees buy houses.'

'What would I do with a whole house? It would only make me feel lonelier.'

'What about Sam? You must see him a lot.'

'Sam is busy procreating like the rest of you.'

You get up to look more closely at our books.

You have no idea. My body relaxes slightly. I thought perhaps that's why you'd come.

Silas thinks I should tell you. And here is my chance, right here. For a long time I said nothing out of anger. I punished you with the only weapon I had, silence. Now I feel like I would hurt you more by telling you. You don't seem strong enough for it somehow.

You study all the books by Churchill—the histories, the memoirs, the letters, the speeches, the poetry—for a long time and make no comment.

On a table beside the shelves are a few framed photographs. You lift up the one of my mother.

'Silas said she died. I didn't know that.'

'It was a long time ago.'

'Not that long.'
'Nine and a half years.'
'He said it was sudden.'
'It was. She went to Chile on vacation and she came back crumbled up in a box.'

He winces at this. 'I'm so sorry.'

'I know she would have liked the quick painless exit. It was definitely her style. But selfishly I wanted a goodbye. A real goodbye.'

I took that photo of my mother. She's on her deck in Phoenix, squinting in the sun, waving a hand at the camera. At the edge of the picture, on the chair beside hers, is the lumbar cushion she'd bought me for the back pain I had during the last trimester.

'Why didn't you call me?' you say in nearly a whisper.

'When?'

'When your mother died.'

'I don't know.'

'I guess you'd met Silas by then.'

'I met him six months later. I was a wreck. But he understood.'

'I wish you'd called me.'

Above us I can hear Silas and the boys, their bedtime noises, bickering, giggling. One of us tells them a story every night. Silas has a long-running tale of two hedgehogs. This week they have been stuck on an ice floe in Antarctica.

I see you struggling to say something, another reproach I really don't want to hear. 'I think Silas needs a closer up there. I better go sing some songs to settle them a bit.'

You nod. You understand I'm cutting you off.

'Your room's the first one on the left. Twin bed. Yellow bedspread. Just kidding—it's blue.'

Early the next morning, before anyone else is up, we eat a bowl of cereal and I walk you out to your car. You open the trunk and hand me a book, the one you talked about yesterday, about Iceland and sheep.

I thank you. We hug. You get into your car.

When you roll down the window, I say, 'Drive safely.'

'You know I will.'

We look at each other a bit warily.

Why did you come?

You wait for me to say something else and when I don't, you lift your fingers briefly off the steering wheel and back out of our driveway. I follow you in bare feet and wave in the road until you're gone, then walk back to the house.

I sit on the porch steps and look at the paperback you gave me. It's your copy, a bit worn, the pages swollen, the cover starting to curl back. There's a scrap of paper wedged in the middle of it. I pull it out. It's not addressed to me or anyone. It's just a paragraph. But I recognize it immediately. It's the Céline passage you read me that time. I don't know if you meant for me to see it. The handwriting is messier than in your letters.

I read it.

> We kissed. But I didn't kiss her properly as I should have, on my knees if the truth be known. I was always partly thinking about something else at the same time, about not wasting time and tenderness, as if I wanted to keep them for something magnificent, something sublime, for later, but not for Molly and not for this particular kiss.

It goes on about his fear that life would steal away in the night with everything he longed to know about it, while he was expending his passion kissing Molly.

> I wouldn't have enough left, I'd have lost everything for want of strength, and life—Life, the true mistress of all real men—would have tricked me as it tricks everyone else.

I read it over several times. You have your regrets and I have mine. I sit on the porch step for a while, thinking about life's tricks, the ones we see, the ones we don't.

Silas' car comes in the driveway. He gets out holding a pint of blueberries, adorable in his short-sleeved work shirt.

'What about your meeting?'

'It was moved to later. Blake came in with these from his farm and I got this craving for pancakes.'

'The boys will be ecstatic.'

He looks down at the book and the paper in my hand. 'He's gone?'

'He's gone.'

'Good guy.'

'That's what he said about you.'

'I liked him,' Silas says. 'You didn't—'

'No. I didn't.'

'Someday.'

'Someday. Maybe.'

He puts out his hand and I take it. He pulls me up to standing and we go inside to make the pancakes.

III

# Thursday

Jack is a liar when it comes to pain. He'll say it's a two when it's a five, a five when he can barely speak. If it's really bad, he'll hand over his book and let one of us read it to him. It's been bad for a week straight now.

Harry is doing his algebra homework at the kitchen table, headphones clamped tight, and Silas is making things sizzle and smoke in the wok. Jack and I are on the couch we moved in here for days like these. He leans heavily against me. I'd prefer to read him stories with no peril and happy endings, but he wants facts. I hold the book with one hand and rub his head with the other and read from a chapter about the mass extinction of mammals on each continent soon after the arrival of the first *Homo sapiens*.

'When the first Americans marched south from Alaska into the plains of Canada and the western United States, they encountered mammoths and mastodons, rodents the size of bears, herds of horses and camels, oversized lions and dozens of large species the likes of which are completely unknown today,' I read. Among these were saber-toothed cats and eight-ton ground sloths as tall as twenty feet. And despite thriving for more than thirty million years, most of these large mammals would be gone forever in two millennia, obliterated by us.

 Jack is wearing a hat Claudette knit for him with three magnets stitched into it, one at the forehead and one at each temple. She's read a lot about magnetic therapy. He says it helps. As he listens, he presses the right-side magnet hard to his skull. I feel it happening before it happens. I feel it on my skin and Jack's skin, a sudden squall, everything dimming. Silas, I think I say but I'm not sure. Jack's body goes soft as if he's just dozing off, then every muscle clenches hard all at once, his arms and legs stiff as wood, and I hold him close to me as he bucks and jolts, his head knocking my jaw, catching my tongue, and I am saying we are on the couch, we are on the couch, because the last time he was alone in the bathroom but here we are okay, we are okay, I am saying, and everything is electric but dark and Harry has pulled his headphones down around his neck and Silas is on the couch with us, holding us both and wiping the blood from where it has dripped out of my mouth. Jack is limp again in my arms. He opens his eyes. The scene is familiar to him, the pallor of our faces, the afterfeeling. He once compared it to Pompeii, waking up and seeing us covered in ash. For it is we who are stunned in place now, he who must wait for our return. His seizures are a response to the pain, and a relief from the pain. He will be an actual two for at least a few days.

'It's all right. I'm good.' He lifts his head up slowly from my lap. I can feel the small aftertremors in his muscles. He reaches for the book that has fallen to the ground. 'Let's keep going, yeah?'

Harry swings his headphones back up and Silas gives us a few more squeezes before he rescues the food on the stove. I try to find my place in the book.

'I want that surgery,' Jack says.

Just after his eighth birthday, Jack began to lose his balance. He said his legs felt weird. They found three gliomas in his brain. He's had three surgeries, but they haven't been able to remove all the tumor tissue. What remains still causes pain and seizures. It's pressing on the brain stem. The doctors down in Boston have recommended we go to Houston for this next one, to a surgeon who specializes in this particular high-risk procedure. We've been on her wait list for five months.

We've spoken to her once, this surgeon. On the phone she was brusque. She preferred to speak directly to Jack, even when Silas or I asked a question. She made lame jokes that Jack loved. 'Now I hate to tell you, but you won't be able to drive a car for six months.' Jack is twelve. I don't have a good feeling about it. But I don't have a good feeling about much of anything these days.

'I know,' I say.

He knows the risks. He has seen it all online. It doesn't matter to him. He is certain he will be fine.

'When they call, I want the first opening. The very first.'

Across the room my phone dings in my bag. We all look at each other.

Harry reaches in, reads the text.

'Who's Sam Gallagher?'

# Friday

It's Silas who insists I go. I hate leaving them, even for a night.

'We'll be fine,' he says, pulling up to the departure doors. Jack has gone to school today, the first time in nine days.

'I know.' But I'm thinking about the surgery. The doctor said they might only give us a day to get to Houston for pre-op.

'Even if we got the call right now, we could get there by Sunday.'

We don't talk about the costs anymore, the unpaid time he's taken off teaching, or the fact that I haven't published anything in five years.

I nod and pull my small suitcase from the back.

'It's just one night,' he says, hugging me outside the revolving doors. 'I'm so sorry,' He means about Yash, but I can only feel the sadness of leaving them.

'I don't want to go,' I say, his arms still around me, my lips against the stubble of his neck. 'I hate hospitals so much.'

\* \* \*

On the plane I hold the rock Jack gave me. He has done this since he was very young, given me a little rock to travel with. He collects them. I've gotten this one before. It has a little dimple in it. Jack calls it heart-shaped but that seems like a stretch. It fits nicely in my hand. We lift off, level out. I watch the clouds out the window. I think of my mother when I'm on a plane. I think of her many places, even though she's been gone sixteen years now. She never knew my boys, but she has helped me raise them. I know how much she loves them. I feel that. I talk to her. I pray to her. I shut my eyes now and beg her to keep them all healthy and safe while I'm away.

I can do this, I think, lifting my cranberry seltzer off the tray table.

It will be fine, I think, my suitcase gliding beside me from the gate to the exit. I bought this roller for my last book tour and I've barely used it since. It's one of the nicest things I own, with its four pert wheels and heavy zippers that don't break. It's navy blue and so responsive and agile it can do pirouettes at the slightest touch. It could run off and join the ballet.

It will be fine, I think, on the highway heading toward the hospital. I can do this. I check my phone. Nothing from home.

In the lobby, I falter. I sink into an armchair facing the elevator bank. My suitcase comes to a reluctant stop by my knee. I can't do this. The elevator cars roar up and wheeze down.

I let a few more minutes go by. When I get up and push the top button, a door slides open immediately. No one inside. My suitcase leaps over the threshold ahead of me. I have to follow it. I press 5.

Sometimes time has a resistance, like a wind. It takes a while for the floor to push against my feet and lift me up.

I don't want to be here. I don't want to do this. I need to be home. I check my phone again. No messages. No call from the surgeon.

The elevator shudders to a stop. The door opens. Ahead is a long hallway that wraps around a nurses' station. The smell hits me. God, I hate that smell.

I look at the text from Sam again, check the room number. 508. I try to bypass the nurses' station, but one of them looks up from her monitor.

'Yash Thakkar?'

How does she know?

I nod.

She points to the corner room diagonally across from where we are. And there is Sam, his back to me, leaning against a wall beside the door and talking to several older women. It's confusing. He has not aged, at least not from the back. A full head of that copper hair, no thinning at the crown, not even a speckle of gray. The same straight spine, narrow waist, bowed legs. One of the women lifts her face to me as I come closer. Sam turns around and becomes a boy. A teenager, Harry's age. Out of room 508 comes another Sam, smaller, younger. He stands there a moment, then his head falls against his brother's shoulder. They move past me, faces crumpled, down the hallway.

'Oh,' the woman gasps, 'Jordan.' She grips my arm. 'You look just the same.'

I have not been called Jordan by anyone but Yash in twenty-eight years.

'It's Rosemary,' she says, 'Rosemary Gallagher.' Sam's mother.

'Rosemary,' I say, unexpectedly moved that she would be here.

She squeezes my hands hard with sharp bones and gold rings. 'You came.'

'Jordan,' the woman to her left says. I recognize her kind smile. Paige, Yash's stepmother. Her hair is short now, her clothes soft and loose as she hugs me. Yash's father died a few years ago, and Yash and Paige are closer now. 'Oh,' she says, 'this will mean the world to him.'

I don't know why they are making such a fuss.

'Go in,' Rosemary says. 'Go see him.'

I move to the door but someone is coming out. It's Yash's mom. 'Oh, honey. You're here.' She is so small. I have to bend down to hug her. Her face, her bones are tiny. She is so frail in my arms. 'He's been waiting for you.'

She pushes open the door. I'm not ready. I'm not ready for any of this.

The room is large and full of people, all men. Eight or ten of them in chairs, a few others standing, all staring at the TV suspended on the far wall. Something happens and they yell at the TV all at once. A few jump to their feet. Yash is in the center, tilted upright in bed, wearing a Georgia Bulldogs cap with the tag still on and yelling with the rest of them.

He's the only one who sees me come in. His face lights up like it used to. Then he sees me take in the oxygen cannula and the IV bags and the Foley catheter coming off the side of his bed, and he remembers where we are and looks at me apologetically.

He holds out his hand and I take it. I take Yash's hand.

'I didn't think you'd come.'

'Of course I came.'

'But Jack.'

'He's fine.'

I bend over and hug him gently, not wanting to displace anything. His mother shoos one of the guys out of a chair and drags it over to me. She glides my suitcase into the corner.

'You sit right here beside him, hon.'

I sit. Yash takes both my hands in his. We haven't touched in this way since Paris. There's another eruption of hollering at the TV.

'It's March Madness.' His whole face is alight again. 'Isn't this amazing?'

I'm having trouble finding my voice. 'It's great,' I say. There's so much noise he can't hear how wobbly it is. 'How are you feeling?'

'I'm good.' He squeezes my hand again. 'I'm so good. You're here. Everyone's here.'

I force myself to look around the room, to identify Sam. Would he speak to me? Would I speak to him? None of the men in the room seems to be him. Brent and Arlo and Yash's Uncle Percy greet me with quick hugs during a break in play for a foul shot. Brent takes a call and leaves the room, finger in his other ear.

'You missed Bean. He was here this morning. He'll be back, though. Isn't this amazing?' Yash says again, glancing around the chaos of the room. 'You see that, Jimmy? I told you. Nothing but bricks from that guy.'

Jimmy agrees.

Yash turns back to me. 'Can you believe this? All these people. I feel so blessed.'

I look at the place where the PICC line goes under the skin on his chest. I wonder how much morphine they're giving him. 'Blessed' is not a word I've ever heard Yash use.

'Do you have a date yet, for the surgery?'

I don't remember telling him about this. That he is capable of recalling it, having concern about it, makes my throat ache. I shake my head.

'You should be home with your family.'

'I should be right here.' This feels more true than I thought it would.

We squeeze our hands tight and look at each other for a long time without speaking, as if this were all normal, this open raw affection between us.

Yash's mom comes in and hands me a cup of tea. 'Do you remember my sister Sue?' She pulls in Yash's aunt, looking just as I left her in Knoxville, from the doorway.

'Of course. I also remember the best piece of pecan pie in my life.' I stand and give her a hug. I offer her my chair.

She waves it away. 'You sit. You're the guest of honor.'

'I'm not. I'm an interloper.' I point to the chair again.

She smiles and shakes her head. 'Thank you for being here.' Her eyes shimmer. 'We'll talk later.'

They go back out into the hallway. Yash reaches for my hands.

'Why is everyone being so nice to me?' I ask.

He doesn't answer because someone has scored a three-pointer to tie it up.

A nurse comes in, to shush everyone, I assume. Instead, she just weaves between all the guys standing and sitting and reaches Yash's other side and swaps out a bag from the IV pole and punches some buttons and adjusts his cannula. She taps a long white fingernail on the oxygen number on the vitals monitor.

'Deep breaths or we'll have to get out the mask.'

He sucks in hard and the numbers go higher.

'Good boy.' She looks at me. 'We want him in the nineties, okay?'

I nod and she leaves and Yash takes my hand again and stares at me.

He was never a hand-holder or an eye-gazer. But somehow it is not uncomfortable.

'I'm so happy, Hink,' he says. 'I've missed you so much.'

We didn't stay in touch after his visit to Maine. Or I didn't. He sent us a thank-you note. He wrote me a letter or two. Maybe more. Things blur after Jack got sick. About a year ago, he called and told me he had cancer. Jack was recovering from his third surgery. We talked a lot that spring and summer. I put him in touch with Jack's oncologist, who recommended someone in Atlanta. Yash had chemo, radiation, then he was placed in a clinical trial and the tumors in his lungs started shrinking. Within a few months one disappeared entirely. He texted me a listing for a small house outside of Atlanta. Below it he wrote, *This worker bee just bought a house!*

That fall I was invited to Boston University to give an evening reading and visit the graduate fiction workshop beforehand. The workshop was taught by the writer Ray Hart. 'The Last Fall' had been Ray Hart's first story to appear in print. Since then, he'd published two perfect novels, twelve years apart. The first I'd read in Phoenix, when I was living with my mother. I wasn't writing then, but when I finished it I told my mother that I was going to write a novel. I keep that book on my desk at all times, to remember that feeling. I'd stopped traveling for work, stopped accepting any kind of invitation years ago, but this wasn't far and I had to go meet Ray Hart.

I called Yash while I was driving down to BU that afternoon. He'd come to love Ray Hart's novels, too, and admitted upon rereading it that even 'The Last Fall' was a good story. It was one of those sharp sparkling October days. Even the highway was beautiful. Jack had gone to school and I was dressed and out of the house, being a professional writer again. Yash was the one person who would understand exactly how thrilling this moment was to me.

He answered on the first ring. I knew right away something was wrong.

The latest tests indicated that the tumors were growing again. The immunotherapy had stopped working. They had already taken him off the drug.

'After one scan? What if it was a fluke? What if they start shrinking again next month?'

'It's a clinical trial. One strike and you're out.'

'What did your doctor say?'

'He told me to tell people. Six months, is what he said.'

'No. I don't believe it. There's got to be something else.'

'Yeah,' I can hear the smile in his voice. 'I thought that's what you'd say.'

His phone bounced like he was walking. I could hear how short his breaths were. 'Where are you?'

'In my empty house. I haven't even gotten a couch yet.'

'You need a couch.'

I heard him sit down somewhere. 'A flight of stairs is like a triathlon for me.' He paused. 'Otherwise I'm just fine.'

I drove on through the sparkling day in a pair of new suede boots, bought for this moment, and felt as if a chasm of years had opened between us, me still young, and him an old man.

He regained his breath and said he was worried about his books. He didn't want them to be separated. His voice split. Was he crying? He never cried. I didn't think I could bear it. But he didn't cry. He just said again that he worried no one would be able to take his books all together. This thought made his breathing worse and I wanted to say I would take them but I did not.

Instead I insisted there would be a new trial, a better drug. I said I would come visit soon, when things with Jack were more stable.

I walked to the university and found my way to the building on my itinerary, up to the classroom where the workshop was held. A few students were already there and I introduced myself and we chatted about their program. Ray Hart was the last to arrive and shut the door behind him.

'She's not here yet?' he said, and a few of them pointed to me.

'Ah, fantastic. Sorry.' He came over and I stood up and we shook hands. 'What a pleasure,' he said. He was holding a few books, two of them mine, in a way that boys in college held them, against his hip. He wore old corduroys with the little ridges worn off at the butt. Everything reminded me of the college boy in his short story, even though he was over sixty now.

He offered me the highbacked chair at the head of the seminar table that was clearly meant for him, and I said I was fine where I was. He smiled and took his place and I could tell the students liked him, that he created an easy atmosphere in that room.

He began by saying he was grateful I was there, that he had admired my work since my first novel. He held up my most recent book and said it was one of the most astonishing things he'd read in years. His words made my chest burn. 'I assigned it to this class two weeks ago and my inbox has been full of something I'm not used to receiving: thank-you notes. From these kids right here. Several confessed they'd never finished a book I assigned before this one. So, you have a captive audience for whatever nuggets of gold they can get out of you.'

He smiled warmly at me. I was stunned by his unexpected praise. We'd had no contact before this moment. I'd been invited by a committee, and all my interactions had been with an administrative assistant. I didn't know he'd read a book of mine, and he had no idea of my attachment to his work.

I thanked him, my voice weakened by a swift clustering of feelings, and I tried to tell the story of discovering his work in college—but what came to mind was the photocopied pages beneath the back door of the Breach and Yash in the tree with my boys, all of them strong and healthy then, and Yash on the phone, upset about his books. I couldn't tamp it all down. It got away from me so quickly. I began to cry at that seminar table and I could not stop. Ray Hart looked at me with horror and I could not explain about Jack, about Yash, about my love for Ray's work and the great surprise of his kindness about mine, which I had all but given up on since Jack got sick. I kept holding up my hand, trying to reassure them I would collect myself in a moment.

    I did eventually regain a bit of composure. To try to explain would unleash another episode, so I fell back on routine sentences about my novels and my process. I showed them the spiral notebooks with my first drafts written in pencil, and I answered their questions as best I could. After the class Ray Hart assigned a student to walk me over to the hall where I'd be speaking. When he introduced me on stage an hour later, I didn't feel the warmth he'd had earlier for my work, but perhaps by then my shame was distorting things. At the dinner afterward we sat on opposite ends of the table, and I had to excuse myself before dessert, to make the drive back to Maine. In the car, I told myself I would write him to explain and apologize, but I never did. Once I got back on the highway I wanted to call Yash again and tell him what a fiasco it had been, meeting Ray Hart. But it was late and I did not want him to know, by telling him about all the crying at the seminar table, that I knew he was dying.

\* \* \*

Something happens on the TV that isn't good and the guys in the hospital room are grumbling.

'There was a ridiculous line down there,' someone says behind me, coming through the door.

My body tenses before my mind catches up.

Sam.

'All the residents and interns who haven't slept for days needing another hit,' he says.

I have a strong impulse to pull my hand out of Yash's.

A coffee in each hand, he rounds the corner at the foot of Yash's bed and goes around to his other side. I notice a chair there in the corner, a backpack beside it. That is his spot. I didn't see it earlier. He places the cups on the cluttered tray attached to the railing on his side. Without looking up, he collects the bunched napkins, empty straw sheaths, and to-go containers and tosses them in a bin behind him. He plucks a tissue from the bedside table, dips it into a cup of water, and wipes down the tray, lifting the new cups of coffee one at a time to clean under them, too.

Yash holds my hand tighter. He can tell I want to let go, not get caught. 'What's happening?' Sam says, and looks right at me.

He has aged, but not all that much. Same hazel eyes. Same small grin.

'Oh, wow. Jordan,' he says.

He comes back around to my side and I get up.

We hug. I can feel him shaking.

'It's so good you came,' he says.

We turn at the same time to look at Yash. He is beaming.

On the TV someone scores and there is cheering. Yash tries to sit up straighter, which pulls the cannula out of his nose, and Sam and I reach to adjust it. Yash takes my hand again.

'Do you want more ice?' Sam says, jiggling Yash's oversized plastic cup.

'No, no. Sit and watch the end of the game.'

Sam sits in his chair in the corner. His head tips back against the wall. He's looking at the TV but not watching it. Within seconds his eyes shut.

'Do you know he has slept here every night for a week?' Yash says. 'Apparently I called him in the middle of the night speaking gibberish. He knew it was my oxygen. He drove over and brought me here. They said I would have died if he hadn't. Every night they set up a little cot for him right there at the foot of my bed.' He shakes his head, giving up on words. Water rises in his eyes then recedes. 'He's been such a friend to me, Hink.'

Sam's boys come in and go around to their father's chair. The younger one pushes his way in between Sam's knees, tugs gently on his sleeve. 'Dad.'

Sam startles. Opens his eyes.

'Mom's here.'

'Okay. Okay. Get your bags.'

'We have them.' They both have backpacks on their shoulders.

Sam nods. He stands and hugs them. The older one is taller than him. 'Are your uniforms at Mom's?'

They say they are and turn to Yash.

'Goodbye, tadpoles,' Yash says.

'Goodbye, toad,' the older one says.

The younger one opens his mouth but nothing comes out. His brave face collapses. He bends over the railing and lays his head on Yash's chest. Yash strokes his hair.

'We can't come tomorrow,' the bigger one says.

'Then I'll see you Sunday,' Yash says. 'I'll be right here. Okay?'

The little one straightens up.

'You get your science quiz back yet?'

He nods.

'And?'

'Ninety-eight.'

'I told you. Did I not tell you?'

He nods again and follows his brother out.

I've never known anything about Sam's children or Yash's relationship with them. He always claimed his friends abandoned him once they had kids.

Outside in the hallway the younger boy is sobbing.

Sam and I look at each other. I'm sorry, I try to say to him with my eyes. I'm sorry you can't protect them from this.

'They're good boys,' Yash says quietly.

Paige leans in from the doorway. 'Rosemary says the doctor on rounds is down the hall.'

Rounds. Wasn't it early for rounds? I look at the clock. Somehow it's past five. I can't account for this.

'Can you put the game on in the family room?' Yash says.

'Ted's doing that right now,' she says.

Yash turns to Sam. 'Time to get everyone out.'

Sam is already reaching for the remote. He cuts the sound and they all seem to know what to do. They high-five Yash on the way out.

I wait for them all to file out, then stand to leave, too.

'Not you, Jordan.' Sam says. Then more softly, 'Would you stay?'

'Of course.' I sit back down, take Yash's hand.

The doctor comes in followed by a flock of residents who quickly settle in a semicircle behind him. Yash and Sam are unfazed by this sudden array of strangers in the room.

'Good afternoon, Mr. Thakkar,' the doctor says without inflection, looking down at his iPad. He lifts his head abruptly and thrusts out his hand. 'Dr. Gaucher.'

Yash releases my hand to shake his.

The doctor turns to me. 'Mrs. Thakkar.'

None of us corrects him. I shake his dry hand.

'How are you feeling today, sir?' Dr. Gaucher says, with more pep than he seems to have in him.

'Good,' Yash says. 'I feel great.'

'Any pain or discomfort, on a scale of one to ten, one being the least amount of pain?'

'Zero,' Yash says.

I feel him trying to please the doctor, get his aid, by being such a good, pain-free patient.

The doctor places the coin of his stethoscope on Yash's chest. 'Seems like you're breathing okay.'

'Yes.'

'And you're getting enough morphine?' He looks at all of us for the answer.

Yash and Sam nod.

'Good,' the doctor says, scrolling on his iPad. 'That's all very good.'

What about any of this is good?

On the other side of the room the residents strain to stay focused. They flex their jaw muscles, shift their weight. Their eyes travel around the room but never to our faces. I study theirs, one at a time. I wonder what dramas have played out among them. I can feel their youth in the room, a forcefield of energy and fear and longing and confusion. I can feel it so strongly. And

I know they sense nothing about us, two men and a woman in our late forties, none of our old entanglements or the freakishness of the three of us being in this room together now.

We are all caught in this performance, Yash pretending that he isn't dying, Sam and the doctor that medicine still has something to offer him, and me in the role of devoted wife at his bedside.

Sam asks him a few questions about oxygen, liters per minute, a medication I don't recognize.

The doctor answers them. 'Anything else?' he says and glances at his watch. Several residents do the same.

*Keep 'em alive until 6:05.* An old med school refrain.

We shake our heads no.

'It's nice to see you have family around you,' he says. 'Not everyone does.' He leaves, the flock close behind.

Sam's phone vibrates and he pulls it out of his pocket. 'It's Cole.'

Yash shakes his head. 'Not again.'

'He says he can't get here till Tuesday now.'

'And he wants to know if I'll be dead by then?'

Sam's laugh is still soundless. 'More or less.'

Yash is pressing on the skin below his collarbone. 'Feel this,' he says.

Sam touches the spot on his chest.

'Push down.'

Sam pushes.

'It's spongy, right?'

'Kind of. That new?'

'I think so. Feel it,' he says to me, spreading open his blue hospital gown wider for me.

I push down on the spot. His bare chest surprises me. I forgot its barrel shape, its smoothness. The spot feels like a small balloon, taut but not dense.

'Should I call him back in here?'

'Let's see if it goes away.'

Sam nods. 'Shall I bring back the horde?'

'Sure.'

Sam goes down to the family room and Yash squeezes my hand. 'You see my cousin Jared, with all the hair? Aunt Sue and Uncle Percy's grandson?'

'That was *Jared*?'

'I worry about that kid. Remember how his parents were supposed to come back and take care of him? They never did. Aunt Sue has had her hands full with him. He wants to be a graphic novelist.' Yash rolls his eyes. 'He wants to move to LA. He's got some friend who knows people, supposedly. It's all a lark. Will you talk some sense into him?'

'How do you mean?'

'He doesn't have a clue. He's just all up here.' He waves a hand above his head. 'He's not being practical. There's some girl out there he'll probably get pregnant.' He sees my expression change, misinterprets. 'Sorry, some very smart young woman. Just talk to him, will you? I worry about him. And I can't help him anymore.'

'Okay. I'll talk to him.'

'Thank you. Tell him what's what. Tell him how hard it is, the creative life. The risks you have to take. Tell him about all the people you know, including me, who don't make it.'

What do you know about taking risks, I want to ask him. You played it so safe. Mr. Cautious. And I protected you the one time things went off the rails.

It is an unpleasant feeling, having this anger at someone who is dying.

The horde returns along with new visitors, people coming straight from work. Two coworkers from the mayor's office, a law school friend, a neighbor. I give up my chair. Jared's back in the room but the chairs around him are all taken. Sam waves me over to his side. We lean against the far wall together.

I'm aware of how much blame I placed on him for everything that happened between me and Yash. All this time I suspected he'd been intent on sabotaging us from the start, lording his moral superiority over Yash, and scoring his final victory by luring him to Atlanta. But standing here beside Sam, who has probably not left this building in seven days, who has been only grateful and kind to me since I arrived, I see it might not have been so simple a story.

Beside him now, I actually *feel* like Jordan again. I feel so young, like I've been shot through a secret portal straight back in time.

'Look at this.' Sam hands me his phone. On the screen is a post on the Facebook page he created for Yash. It's a long passage by someone named Connie about going to K-Mart with Yash in eighth grade to get materials for a project and how funny he was just picking out magic markers and how after that she had a mad crush on him but he never knew.

I laugh and hand back his phone.

'There's one like this every few hours. All the unrequited crushes on Yash Thakkar.'

Uncle Bill gets up, which leaves a free chair beside Jared.

'Excuse me,' I say to Sam and push myself off the wall. 'Yash has given me an assignment.'

I slip into the empty seat. 'Jared, right?' I say. 'You probably don't remember, but we once played Red Light Green Light in your driveway.'

'I remember.' He tries to smile. His eyes are a mess. He swipes at his nose. 'You had a side ponytail and called me a tater tot.'

'Side ponytail. Impressive vocab. My husband is still shaky on the difference between a dress and skirt.' One of Yash's aunts lifts her head in my direction. It feels strangely unfaithful to mention a husband in here.

'I draw people. So I have to know these things.'

'Yash says you want to write graphic novels?'

'I've written two. Nearly done with the third. It's a sort of a triptych.'

'Has anyone seen them yet?'

'Yeah. I have an agent. She's waiting for the last one before she goes out with it.'

'And you're moving to LA?'

'I was supposed to be out there for interviews today and tomorrow at Pixar—I have a friend who works there—but I pushed them till next week. They've been cool about that.' He looks at Yash, who's talking to Sam and someone in a coat and tie who has just come in. 'He's like my dad or my brother, or both, really. I have to be here.'

This is the kid Yash was worried about?

'He wants the very best for you.'

'He thinks I'm a loser.'

'No, he doesn't.'

'He does. He thinks my dreams are too big, that I'm in the clouds, drifting around.'

'It's more about him than you. He's a worrier.'

He nods. 'I know it's out of concern. I just need to get to California. There's a girl there. We're not together or anything.'

'But you're going out to woo her.'

He leans back and tries to say something.

I wait.

'I'll probably be too sad to woo,' he says with a lot of effort.

I pat his knee a few times. He has no idea how appealing an adorable big-haired grieving guy can be. 'When you're ready, you're going to woo her socks off.'

'Jesus,' Yash says. 'I said talk to him, not make out with him.' The new people have gone and I've got my chair back. 'You are not to be trusted, even at my deathbed.'

'Jared's going to be fine.'

'You think?'

'Totally.'

'We'll see. I'm leaving what I have to him. Not that it's much. A very small nest egg.'

We're silent for a bit.

'Do you think I'll know everything soon?'

My stomach turns over. I can't meet his gaze and look down at our hands. 'Probably.'

'I'll finally find out about that guy in Spain,' he says.

I had a few boyfriends after Yash and before Silas, but I've only ever mentioned Paco. I was with Paco when Yash sent me the elephant poem.

'I'll tell you about that guy in Spain right now.'

Yash holds up his hand. 'No. Don't. I'll wait for the EP afterlife version. All the gory details.'

'Well, he'll be the one with his sweaters tucked into his gray jeans.'

Yash laughs. 'I knew he was a dweeb.'

'It was a very cool look back then.'

'Yeah, right.'

I notice his oxygen has dipped. I press the cannula back into his nostrils. 'Take some deep breaths.'

'Deep is relative,' he says. I model some big breaths. He watches and imitates me as best he can and gets it back up to 93. He continues to stare at me.

It's hard to return his gaze, the way he is looking at me. 'You are so beautiful, babe,' he says.

*Babe.* A word from another universe. It's physically disorienting.

'Yash,' his uncle says from across the room.

But Yash ignores him. He sees I have something on my mind. 'What?' he says. 'What is it?'

But Uncle Percy is louder. 'Listen up, you two love birds. You need to tell us. What do you want for dinner? I cannot put another carton of pork lo mein in my delicate stomach,' he says, patting his belly.

'Looks like you have a pig or two in there already,' Yash says.

'I got a barnyard in here, Yashie.'

They decide on Italian.

Aunt Sue offers to go in her car. Jared holds up his phone. He can get it delivered.

'You can't deliver to a hospital,' Uncle Percy says.
Jared explains.
'Jordash?' Uncle Percy says.
'Door Dash,' Jared says slowly.
'Jordash is clothes.'

'I got this,' Jared says calmly, no irritation, then begins taking people's orders.

Yash smiles at me and seems not to remember his last question.

'Love in your novels, I think, acts as a form of hope. Why hope? Do you believe this?'

I was on stage in Reykjavik with my Icelandic editor, Birna Gunarsdóttir. We'd never met before this trip, my last before Jack got sick.

'Most people ask me about sex, not love.'

'I know. I have seen this online. But I want to know about love.'

'Isn't love a form of hope?' I said.

'No. Love is crushing. Love is something you let yourself feel at your own peril, despite your better sense.' She wore all black and bright red lipstick and I saw in her face how serious she was. After a few seconds she forced herself to soften it.

She had the audience's attention.

'True. It's all those things,' I said. 'But where would we be if we didn't feel it? I think it's the only form of hope we have. For our survival, I mean. What good is any other virtue without love?'

'In literature love is a weakness. Othello is easily manipulated by Iago because of his love for Desdemona. Anna Karenina throws herself under a train.'

'Othello places his trust in Iago, not Desdemona. Anna Karenina's society does not allow her to be with Vronsky. Love is not the weakness. People get in its way. People are weak and perilous, not love.'

She pursed her red lips and moved on. 'I have read in several interviews from years ago that *Independent People* is one of your favorite books. Is this true?'

'It is. Maybe my very favorite.'

There was some spontaneous clapping from the audience.

'Why? Why this one about a miserable sheep farmer?'

'You know how you can remember exactly when and where you read certain books? A great novel, a truly great one, not only captures a particular fictional experience, it alters and intensifies the way you experience your own life while you're reading it. And it preserves it, like a time capsule.' Even though nearly everyone in the audience is Icelandic and English is not their first language, I can feel that they are with me. 'When I think of reading *Independent People*, I remember the summer air coming through our windows and the quilt we had on our bed and my boys, so little then. And I remember Silas, my husband, reading it right after I did and we started calling each other Bjartur.' The audience burst out laughing and I figured it was because I'd butchered the pronunciation of his name.

Birna was amused, too. 'You called each other Bjartur? Why?'

'As a term of endearment.'

More laughter.

'I think this has never happened in our country, making a pet name from this hard and complicated character,' Birna said, smiling and shaking her head. 'How did this book come to find you? Most Americans don't know it.'

'A friend gave it to me.' For a moment I was barefoot in our road, watching his car disappear.

I could tell Birna wanted to ask more, but she sensed something and veered away. She smiled, thanked me for coming to Reykjavik, and opened it up to questions from the audience.

When the food delivery is close, I leave the room with Jared and Aunt Bev to help carry up the bags. At the elevator bank I try to give him cash to help him cover dinner, but he won't take it. A door opens and the three of us get in. Aunt Bev is looking at me. I only met one of Yash's aunts in Knoxville, Aunt Sue, not Bev or Mo. I remember him saying one was nice and one was mean.

I'm not sure which Aunt Bev is, but she is glaring at me now.

'You were the one.'

I shake my head.

'You were. He never recovered,' she says. 'And if your books are any indication, he's certainly not the only one you've chewed up and spat out.'

The door opens. I hope to God she's the mean one.

We bring the food up to the family room and set it up buffet-style. A nurse brings us paper plates and utensils. I make plates for Yash and Sam and bring them back to the room. Nearly everyone else has gone down the hall to eat. The room is dim and they are talking quietly. Sam thanks me and tells me to come back with a plate of my own. Yash looks worse. He waves away the food.

In the family room most people have gotten their dinner and are seated in a big ring around the room. As I fill my plate a bald man with a lot of aftershave on tells me the carbonara is good. I thank him and scoop some onto my plate.

'You have no idea who I am, do you?'

I give him a hard stare. I imagine hair on his head. 'Oh my God. EJ?'

He tips an imaginary hat at me. I know that he spent some time in a psychiatric hospital, that he and Marni broke up, that he has a new family now.

'How are you?' I stammer.

'I'm fine. A little beat up over all this. But it's life, right?' He loads his plate with seconds. 'He's just gonna get there a little before the rest of us. I only wish things had been different for him.'

Yash would say the same thing about EJ. 'He's so happy everyone's here.'

'Yeah, everyone's here for a day or two.' We stand with our full plates by the window. 'But you've done well for yourself.'

I hold up my fork. 'Please don't tell me I was the one who got away.'

'You got away all right.'

'I was pushed.'

He shrugs. 'He pushes everyone away at one time or another. It's temporary. You knew that.'

'I didn't. I didn't know that. At the time it felt like the end of the world.'

Sam comes up to us, apologizes for interrupting. 'Can you come back to the room, Jordan?'

'Excuse me, EJ.'

'You go to Yasher. He needs you.'

I follow Sam down the hallway. Outside the room he says, 'He gets this way at night. Really agitated. I've asked the nurse to give him some Ativan. I just—' He looks up to the ceiling. 'Maybe you could go in. Maybe you could, like, sing to him?'

'Sing?'

'You know. Some of your songs. About fairs.' He grins at me.

It's a shock when people remember what you remember. Those few weeks, many, many springs ago, when I sang Sam to sleep. 'Sure.' I don't think I ever sang to Yash.

He opens the door for me and I go in alone. Yash has a terrible look in his eyes. I sit down in my chair and he clutches at me.

'It's not good. It's not good, Hink.' He's shivering.

'The nurse is coming.'

'She won't help.'

'She will. She'll help you sleep. Take some breaths.'

'I can't. I can't take any more breaths.'

'Yes, you can. Do you know about square breathing?'

He shakes his head but looks at me hopefully.

'I do it with Jack. It helps a lot.'

'With the pain?'

'Yeah.'

'That poor kid.'

'It's okay. He's okay.' I don't know if that's true. I don't know how his day has gone. My phone's been in my bag in the corner since I got here. 'You're okay. Here we go. Take a breath in then hold three seconds, then breathe out and hold three more and breathe in again.'

His breaths are so short, so shallow. Maybe it isn't good for him to pause. 'Maybe one-second holds,' I say.

He nods. He reminds me of Jack when it's bad.

And then I'm singing. I sing about sailing away, my own true love. He looks at me with such surprise—You? Singing Dylan?—and I smile and my voice gets steadier. We both relax a bit.

When I sing this song for my boys, it's like a fairy tale, with the mountains and diamonds and western winds. Here with Yash it becomes something different, our own saga of coming and going, of finding and losing each other, of letting go.

I sing and he grips my hands hard and his whole body shudders. I come to the line about wanting the same thing again tomorrow. I barely get it out.

I pause when the nurse comes in with the Ativan. I start up again when she leaves. It's a long song and it's hard to push the words out, each line laden with sorrow and regret. Every image seems like a metaphor for loss. I can't look at Yash. I can only look at his hands in mine. Finally I get to the last lines. Yes, there is something she could bring back to him. Boots of Spanish leather. Yash's eyes are closed and his trembling has died down.

'Lovely,' Sam says quietly.

I turn.

He's in the doorway. He sees my tears and comes to put a hand on my shoulder. It's warm and trembling. We watch Yash sleep.

An orderly rolls in Sam's cot and he helps her set it up at the foot of Yash's bed. He takes out sheets from a cabinet and makes up the bed. When he leans over, his T-shirt rides up and the band of his blue boxers shows above the waist of his jeans like it always did, way before it became a trend.

The clock above the sink says 9:45. I don't know how that's possible. I've missed saying goodnight to Jack. I let go of Yash's hands. It doesn't wake him. I stand up. My back is sore from stretching my arms over the bed railing most of the day. Sam sits on his cot.

'Will he sleep through the night?' I say.

'Mostly.'

'Will you?'

'I think so.' He stands up. 'Do you have an early flight out?'

'I'm going to change it. I'll come back in the morning for a few hours.'

'I'm glad. Maybe we'll have a chance to talk more.'

I hope we don't have that chance. I nod. 'Noche noche, Sam.'

I get my suitcase from the corner and follow it out the door.

In the taxi, I switch my six a.m. flight to noon and text Silas the details. I check in at the hotel and go up to my floor. The hallway is wide and the carpet very plush.

Before Jack got sick we used to travel. The boys loved going to hotels like this, racing down to the room, fighting about whose turn it was to unlock the door. Once inside they investigated every inch: the snacks, the safe, the showerhead. We got room service. We played cards on the bed. We always stayed in one room, two double beds, and I'm not sure I was ever happier than when we were all together in a hotel room.

This one feels very empty. My ears ring in the silence. I turn up the heat and I drop onto the bed with my phone. I call Silas. No answer. Carson and Claudette have texted me messages with a lot of emojis, sending love to me in Atlanta.

I click my screen off. It is black for a few seconds then lights up again. Silas.

'You're still up,' I say. 'Not a good sign.'

'He's okay.'

Silas isn't okay, I can hear that.

'We had a rough patch this evening. But he's asleep now.'

'Real asleep or fake?'

'I think it's real.'

'He's gotten good at faking it.'

'I know.' He's exhausted. I can hear it. He's had to absorb all the emotion because I'm not there to do it. We switch back and forth physically coping with Jack's discomfort, but when we go to bed, I'm the one who holds the worry. Early on, I got angry about this, how he didn't want to talk about it once Jack was asleep, wouldn't listen or try to soothe my anxiety. Finally he told me that he couldn't handle my fears at night, that they scared the shit out of him and he just needed to let it go and sleep. I can tell he's trying hard not to off-load it all on to me tonight.

'How's Yash?'

I planned to tell him everything, from my dread in the lobby to the doctor mistaking me for the wife to singing him to sleep. Was that because I wanted to share the experience with him or to distance myself from the day by making it into a story? I'm too tired to figure it out or say much of anything. 'He got agitated in the evening. It's called breath panic.'

'That sounds awful.'

'It was. That's why I switched my flight, to get a few hours with him tomorrow morning.'

He lets out a long breath. I feel my slight remove from the despair of one of Jack's bad nights.

'It's going to be okay, my love. Tell me about Harry's day.'

'He went to bed early. He has that bio test tomorrow. I think something might have happened with Briar but you'll have to get that out of him.'

'Something good?'

'I think so.'

'Why do you think so?'

'He was texting with that little smile he gets.'

I know just what he means. This makes me happy. He's had a crush on Briar for a long time.

'And he and Murphy did a little fishing off the bridge. To try out that rod they found. Wow, so many sirens there.'

'I'm on the straightaway to the hospital.'

'Are you going to be able to sleep?'

'I don't know.'

'It's good you're there.'

'Bad timing.'

'It was never going to be good timing.'

'I guess not.'

'I miss you.' I can hear him patting my side of the bed.

'I miss you, too,' I say. 'There was this moment today when he asked me if I thought he would find out everything once he was dead and I had this cold wave come over me and I felt like I should tell him.'

'You should,' he says in his clipped, definitive teacher's voice that annoys me.

'Silas.'

'You always said you were going to.'

'*You* always said I was going to,' I say. 'I don't know why it matters to you so much. I told *you* about it.'

He is silent. It hurt him, how long I'd waited. It was a rocky moment in our marriage. I told him because

I was pregnant with Harry, and though I'd lied on the forms, the obstetrician took one look at me and knew. And that felt weird, her knowing and Silas not.

'It matters to me because it matters to you,' he says finally. 'I know it does. It comes up.'

'It comes up and then goes back down.'

'Don't you want to let it go?'

'It's too late. I missed my moment. He'll just be angry and hurt and not have time to process it.'

'You don't know that.'

'I think it might actually kill him.'

'It's not going to kill him.'

'And then everyone will be like, that nasty girl from Maine came and killed our Yashie, and they'll put me in an Atlanta jail for the rest of my life.' I'm speaking with a Southern accent now. I have a very good Southern accent, truth be told.

He laughs but he's not amused. 'You've been given this opportunity. You're not going to get another. Do it for yourself. You've protected him long enough.'

'So weird that you said that. I was thinking that today. I protected him. Why?'

'Because you loved him.'

'It didn't feel like love. I was angry at him. So angry. I wanted to punish him, he who always knew everything.'

'It's going to get in the way of saying goodbye. Just tell him.'

I can hear how tired he is. I have the impulse to launch a real argument, or tirade, about men and their ignorance of women's lived experiences and how we cope with so much they cannot understand, but they always make us feel in some sort of debt. But he might only get a few hours' sleep if Jack has a bad night, and Silas is the exception to the rule, so I let it go.

We say our goodnights and hang up.

As soon as his voice is gone I have that feeling I often have when I'm away from my family, like they are moving farther and farther away from me, beginning to flicker faintly as distant stars and I will never ever reach them again. It feels like a premonition of the fact that someday, one by one, we will be separated from each other forever.

A siren wails past. My remaining hours in this town stretch out before me. Too long and too short.

## Saturday

I wake up in the dark, no light yet at the edges of the thick curtain, surfacing from a dream about trying to find Harry at a restaurant, to give him a message. He was still in a highchair. I saw him through a window, but there was no door.

I reach for my phone to see the time, to see how much more of the night I have to get through, and before I touch it a text from Yash lights up the screen.

*Come as early as you can.*

*Coming.*

Ten minutes later I'm in a cab.

The lobby of the hospital feels like a church, cavernous and empty. The elevator opens instantly and speeds me up to five.

Yash is alone in the room, Sam and his cot are gone. He's holding his phone but the screen is dark. He's fallen back asleep. I tuck my suitcase in its corner and slide a chair quietly to his bedside. When my bracelet clinks against the bedrail, he turns and smiles.

'You're here.' He takes my hand and tucks it with two hands against his breastbone. It strains my back, reaching over the bedrail, but I don't pull away.

'When my cancer came back,' he says, 'yours was the only voice I wanted to hear.'

'Came back?'

'It was minor the first time. At least that was the impression I got.' He shakes his head. 'What's major and minor in life? No one tells you up front. It was a procedure, some radiation. All over in a few months. That's when I went to Maine, after the treatment was over.'

'You didn't tell me.'

'There weren't any friends up the coast. I just didn't want to die without seeing you again.'

'Yash.' I squeeze his hand on his chest tighter and put my other hand on top of it.

'I'm glad we're friends again,' he says. But he's looking at me like we've had a long and intimate life together.

Sam comes through the door with three coffees. Again I have the impulse to pull my hands out of Yash's.

He puts Yash's coffee on his tray and holds up the other two cups. 'Do you drink coffee now?'

'In a pinch.'

'Black?' He holds up the other one. 'Or with milk? I can go either way.'

'No, you can't, Sam.' I laugh. 'Give me the milk.'

'Thank God,' he says with a little grin. Yash was right. His mouth *is* a bit like Silas'. He pushes a button on the side of the bed and Yash is tilted up to sitting.

We drink our coffees. Sam makes Yash laugh with his reports on the most recent Facebook posts.

It's impossible to believe he is dying.

'Remember,' Yash says, 'how Ivan would get us to get him a coffee that he'd give to the nurse he had a crush on?'

'Mona,' Sam says.

'He was on the make till the very end,' Yash says.

Sam is already done with his coffee and picking at the rim of the paper cup. They've done all this before, and now Sam is going to be left alone. I know Yash is thinking the same thing.

I say, 'Remember how Ivan would come over in the morning and spread his arms out like this over the striped couch and say, "I was phenomenal last night. I outdid myself."'

'You sound just like him,' Sam says.

Slowly we go back into the past. Ivan's *Finnegan's Wake* corkboard. Sam's Hume breakdown. I describe walking into the Breach for the first time, the silhouettes above the table by the door, the wallpaper in the bathroom, the drawer of pipes in the study. None of us has thought of these things for so long. I'm careful to stay downstairs—no green bedroom, no etchings, no *Confessions* on the nightstand.

'And those gorgeous wineglasses, paper thin. We used them when we played Sir Hincomb Funnibuster,'

I say and Yash nods with his morphine smile and Sam looks at me blankly.

'The card game.' I wait for him to remember. 'Club the Policeman? Spade the Gardener?'

'Heart the Lover,' Yash says. He is looking at me as if Sam weren't there.

Sam remembers.

Yash says the name of some breakfast place and I shake my head. 'We went there all the time,' he says, but my memory of that year seems limited to the Breach House.

They reminisce about other places, friends of theirs I can't find faces for.

'I remember you getting up at four thirty in the morning to write your short stories,' Sam says.

I laugh. 'The day they were due, no doubt.'

'You'd go into Gastrell's study and come out with a whole story. That was extraordinary to me.'

Did I do that? 'Well, let's say it was not high literature. And you two were the first to tell me so.'

'They weren't that bad,' Sam says.

'Revisionist history! Neither of you ever said anything kind about anything I wrote.'

'The altar boy with the harelip?' Yash says.

We all laugh hard.

'My long Flannery O'Connor stage.'

'But you were doing it,' Sam says.
'The two of you were my real education.'
They look at each other and grin.
'That's not what I mean!' I laugh. And blush. 'You took your minds seriously. I didn't do that before I met you.'
'But Gastrell called you a natural prose stylist,' Yash says.
'What are you talking about?'
'On the bottom of your paper on *The Aeneid*.'
*Someday we will remember even these our hardships with pleasure.* I remember Gastrell closing the book and saying that line with his eyes shut.
'He didn't write that,' I say.
'You guys took his Immortality seminar together?' Sam says.
'How could you forget it?' Yash says to me.
'I always wanted to take that,' Sam says.
'I was a little piqued by it, actually,' Yash says.
'Because all he called you was a genius with the most protean mind he'd ever come across?' I say.
Yash smiles. 'I wanted to be a natural prose stylist.'
'He taught that class at the house, didn't he?' Sam says.
I nod. The striped couch, our feet touching under the coffee table.
'Yeah,' Yash says. 'It was strange.'

Sam nods. He's torn his cup in so many places it looks like a starfish. He tosses it on Yash's tray table. 'I'm going down for another. Any takers?'

We both say no.

It's still quiet on the fifth floor. We can hear his steps fade slowly away down the hallway.

'I didn't want to lose either one of you that fall,' Yash says.

'And you didn't,' I say and we squeeze our hands hard together.

'Not then. But I did lose you.'

'We lost each other,' I say.

'I need to tell you, Hink—'

'Knock, knock,' someone says in the open doorway.

'Jamie's back,' Yash says.

'How're you feeling, Mr. Thakkar?' A nurse in braids and dark blue scrubs comes in.

'I'm great.'

She goes around to his other side and replaces an empty bag hanging on the rack with a full plump one.

'You?' Yash asks.

She pauses what she's doing to shine a big smile at him. 'I'm good, too,' she says and squeezes his shoulder. All in one practiced motion, she detaches a tube by his elbow, attaches a syringe, pushes the plastic lever to the hilt, removes it, and replaces the tube.

When she leaves I see Sam intercept her out in the hallway. I wonder if he's asking her about the air pocket below Yash's collarbone.

Yash's family arrives then, all at once, from the hotel. I try to give up my chair to his mom, to Paige, to Aunt Sue, but they insist I stay right there. They bend over Yash briefly, ask how he slept, glance at the oxygen meter, give him a reassuring pat, then take their places: the men in the chairs around the room and the women outside the door. They settle in like colleagues at the office. This is their work now, this vigil.

Yash takes a long sip of his coffee and shuts his eyes. The room is full of male murmuring. Uncle Bill is sharing his thoughts on supply chain management with Jared. Arlo and EJ are discussing seeds and brackets and perimeter shooting, gearing up for the next round of basketball.

I don't know if I will get him alone again.

Yash opens his eyes. 'Can I tell you a secret, Hink?'

'Tell me.'

'I know you have to go in a few hours, so I just wanted to tell you first. I'm not dying.'

'No?'

'I'm getting better. I can feel it. I feel bad because everyone's here, but I'm not dying anymore. Don't tell anyone yet. I want to enjoy it a little longer, all these people. Is that bad?'

'Of course not.'

'I can tell them tomorrow.'

'All right.'

'But thank you for being here. I'll never forget it. With everything you have going on.' He looks at me with so much concern my eyes get watery. He squeezes my hand. 'He's going to be fine, Hink. He is. We're all going to be fine.'

His mother guides a visitor through the door: pinstriped suit, damp hair, big cup of coffee. I vacate my chair for him, but he recoils from it, says he is just here for a quick visit, he should have been at the office an hour ago, as if Yash has held him up. I take a chair across the room anyway.

'Marco,' Yash says. I can tell he doesn't like him much.

'Hey, buddy,' Marco says as if speaking to an eight-year-old. 'We miss you down there. Nothing's getting done. The place is going to the shitter.'

'Yeah, Sebastian told me he's considering resigning.'

Marco's smile freezes.

'Kidding,' Yash says.

Marco lets out a breath. 'Don't kid a kidder, Yashman.'

Uncle Bill turns on the TV. The local meteorologist drowns out the middle of their conversation. It clicks off after the weather report.

'No, I never wrote more than a few chapters,' Yash is saying.

'You'll do it.'

'Dubious at this point, Marco.'

'You will. I'm going to look for it. I'm going to look for it a year from now.' He looks at his watch. 'Well, I gotta hit it. It's good to see you, buddy.' He shakes Yash's hand. 'Really good to see you.' He backs up. Before he leaves, he smacks the doorjamb a few times then points at Yash. 'I'm going to look for that novel of yours!'

I try making eye contact with Yash, but Yash is still looking at the doorway. His phone lights up and he bends over it.

Every person in this room has a phone in their hand. Arlo is speaking into his loudly. 'That is unacceptable period. Do not move forward exclamation point. Will discuss when I get back'—he lowers his voice slightly—'heart emoji.'

I look at Yash's oxygen. It's flashing between 89 and 91. I get up and reclaim my chair, push his cannula in further.

He says, 'I want to tell you something.'

'Tell me.' I scootch my chair as close as possible to his bed and lean over the bedrail.

He laces his fingers through mine. 'I want to tell you that I'm not angry at you anymore.'

I laugh. He's serious. 'Angry at me?'

'For a long time I felt like you sort of enjoyed making me suffer, punishing me, stringing me'—he pauses to breathe—'along and extracting more and more apologies without ever forgiving me.'

'I remember an elephant poem. And a paragraph about Molly the prostitute—Céline was a Nazi sympathizer, by the way. I don't remember an apology.'

'I apologized so many times. In so many letters.'

Did he? I have no recollection of this. All I remember is other people's writing, other people's thoughts copied out in his hand.

'You thought I was toying with you?' I say.

'I thought it was pretty immature that you wouldn't talk to me for three years when we had been in what to my mind was a pretty serious relationship.'

'Oh. A pretty serious relationship? But not serious enough to show up in New York. More of a drive-in-the-opposite-direction kind of serious.'

'I worried we still couldn't have this conversation.'

'You've never tried to have this conversation.'

'I've tried for years. You have never let me explain.'

'What is there to explain? I was there. You weren't.'

'There were reasons for that.'

'We had something kind of amazing.'

'I know.'

'And you threw it away.'

'I didn't. I didn't mean to. I freaked out. Temporarily. I was twenty-three.'

'I was twenty-three, too.'

There is a flurry of activity in the doorway and three women sweep into the room, sisters maybe, fluffy coats way too warm for Atlanta, their hair streaked blond in the exact same way, dark roots showing intentionally.

'Oh, no way,' Yash says to them.

'Yes fucking way,' the oldest one says.

They crowd around his bed. Big product and perfume smells. I get up and stand in the doorway with his mom.

Yash shakes his head. 'You've come too far.' He looks at me, asking for a truce. 'It's Marni and her girls, Hink.'

Marni. She and I hug, and marvel at her daughters, grown women now. Tears are already sending their mascara down their cheeks. She takes my chair and the girls lean against the bedrail.

'Pigeons,' Yash says reaching out his free hand. 'No fussing about me. I'm fine. I'm really fine.'

This makes them cry harder.

I can't make small talk right now. I feel like my lungs are on fire. I slip out of the room and look for Sam to find out what he talked to the nurse about. He's not around so I keep walking to the bathroom. Yash's posse is spread out over this whole floor. Brent and Aunt Bev are on their computers in the family room. EJ has found a little alcove for a work call, and Jared and Uncle Percy are in the kitchen eating ramen noodles beside the microwave.

In the bathroom stall I look at my phone. Silas has texted. *All good here. Safe flight xo.*

I look at the time. The numbers make no sense to me.

My noon flight has already left.

I call Silas' phone.

'Hello, Madre,' Jack says.

The sound of his voice pushes everything else out of my mind. 'Hello, sweet pea. How's it going?'

'Okay.' He's not in pain but something is preoccupying him.

'What's going on?'

'Nothing.'

I wait.

'I just. I just want to get this *procedure* over and done with.' He says the word 'procedure' the way the Houston doctor said it. Her *procedure* was a seven-hour surgery.

'This will be the last one for a long time.'

'I just—'

'I know.'

'No, I don't think you do know.'

I wait.

'I'm like a ghost in school. Just when I start to sort of be like a regularish kid who actually shows up, I have to leave again. Otis has a girlfriend.'

'Really?'

'Yeah.'

I wait.

'She wears funny shoes.'

'Yeah?'

'Old-fashioned. They're weird. I'm getting behind in everything.'

'In girls, you mean.'

'In girls, in sports, in Spanish. Alex used a word I didn't know today. Pájaro. Do you know what it means?'

'Bird.'

'Even you know it!'

'I did live in Spain.'

'I'm just behind. And I want to go on that trip next year. It's part of the curriculum. You don't have to pay for it.'

'You will go on that trip. I promise.' Please, dear God.

'Do you think it's possible for aliens to come and infect us like a virus with their thoughts?'

'You are not allowed to watch that show.'

'I'm not watching that show. Otis was telling me about it.'

Otis, the kid who told him about the atom bomb in kindergarten, porn in second grade, who never lets Jack's surgeries, pain, or months of absences get in the way of a good friendship. The most loyal, foul-mouthed, naughty, generous friend you could ever wish for.

'What are you at right now?'

'One.'

'Truthfully?'

'Yes.'

'You take your pill?'

'Not yet.'

'Take it before it creeps up on you.'

'How's Yash in the Tree?' That's what my boys call him, Yash in the Tree.

'He's all right. He's not in pain.'

'Morphine?'

'Yeah.'

'Good stuff.'

Not what the mother of a twelve-year-old wants to hear.

'I'll be home later today. Early evening probably.'

'Okay, cool. Otis asked if I want to be a thruple.'

'Wow.'

'You know what that is?'

'Mmhmm.'

'I said no.'

'I think that was wise.'

'I don't want to share my first girlfriend.'
'Or maybe any girlfriend.'
'Down the line I might feel differently.'

Down the line. Oh, this kid of mine. I have to remember this conversation verbatim for Silas.

'Otis says it was her idea. He says she was going to ask me out, then she heard I'd be out of school for a month so she asked Otis instead. They want to come visit me when I'm back.'

'Even if you're not a thruple?'

'Yeah. I hope she wears those shoes. So you can see them. Mom?'

'Yeah?'

'Do you think, really really honestly and not just to keep my hopes up, do you think I'll be able to go on that trip to Mexico?'

'I do. I really, really do.' And I do. It is my job to believe that, to know that, with my whole heart.

'I forgot to brush my teeth this morning. And last night.'

'You should go do that after we hang up.'

'I can feel crud stuck in places.' He is moving his tongue across his teeth. 'Did Yash say that thing about his teeth being shelves for food?'

'Yes.'

'I think about that a lot.'

'Me too.'

'You do have teeth like that. You always have food in them.'

I laugh. 'It's a problem. I should probably get braces.'

'You wouldn't, would you?'

'You don't want a mother with braces?'

'Mom.'

'I could get the invisible kind, that look like plastic wrap and make you slur your words a little.'

'*Mom.*'

'I won't. Can you tell Dad I'll be on a later flight? And I'll grab a cab.'

'Okay. I'm going to let you go now.'

I laugh. He's imitating Silas' mother. 'Brush your teeth. I love you.'

I stay in the stall and book a flight for early evening.

Outside 508 Marni comforts her girls. 'They had to put a mask on him and we couldn't talk to him after that,' she says.

She comes closer and says to me quietly, 'God, he looks dreadful.'

Does he? I can't see that anymore. I nod anyway.

She takes my hand. I've never done so much hand-holding in my life.

'It's good you're here.' She looks at her watch. 'Oh shit. We have to go.'

'We need to say goodbye,' one of the pigeons says.

'We will.' She opens the door and they disappear through it.

I go back down the hallway and sit in the alcove that EJ has vacated. Was he hiding from Marni? Two nurses are nearby, chatting near the opening of their station where they come in and out. They are talking quietly about someone named Kelly. She never takes the tray, she sees it but she never takes it, so annoying. I sit there motionless, numb, knowing Marni and her girls are doing what I will have to do in a few hours. I don't understand Marni coming for fifteen minutes. It makes no sense. None of it makes any sense.

I return to the room. Yash has a mask on. His oxygen is at 96. Sam is poking his neck.

Yash puts his hand out to me. 'Feel that,' he says, a bit muffled through the mask. He tilts his neck for me to poke too.

My finger sinks in, worse than before.

Sam's phone buzzes. He looks at the screen. 'He's on his way.'

'I'm inflating,' Yash says.

'We'll ask the doctor.'

'Who's on the way?' I say.

'His boss,' Sam says.

The DA arrives in the doorway in a charcoal suit without a crease. He is tall and striking. Yash has said he's planning a run for Congress. Yash has been writing his speeches. I vacate my chair but he doesn't sit. He shakes Yash's hand then rests his forearms on the bed railing and says, 'Well, this sucks.' He speaks like a voiceover.

Yash lowers his mask. 'It's not optimal.'

'I'm sorry.'

'You've seen worse. I know that. How did it go?'

'Yesterday?'

'Yeah.'

'Putty in my hands. I stole your line about not one good deed but the habit of goodness.' His voice is mesmerizing.

'I might have borrowed a tad from Aristotle.'

The DA nods twice. Then his face splits open. The smooth veneer cracks. He bends down closer and speaks quietly in a deep murmur. 'I will never work with anyone as gifted again, Yash Thakkar. No one will ever come close. It's been an honor and a privilege.'

'The privilege has been mine, sir,' Yash says.

They clasp hands for longer than I expect.

I signal to Yash that his oxygen is too low.

'Pull yourself together, councilor, and go work the room.' Yash says, and tugs his mask back up over his mouth and nose.

The DA moves slowly around the perimeter, introducing himself, repeating each name. He gives Yash's mom a hug.

When he gets to me, I tell him my name and he says, 'I have all your books.'

I look at Yash. 'You foisted them on him, too?'

I see a smile beneath his foggy mask.

'I'm a fan. The one about the musicians? Loved it.'

The DA moves on. Yash is feeling his neck again. It is swelling. How like him to complain about his job for years, when it turns out he is utterly revered by the boss.

He lowers his mask. 'Do I look like a frog?'

I shake my head.

'I do. I look like a frog.'

Sam taps my shoulder and gestures for me to step out of the room with him. I follow him down the hallway. He stops and leans against a wall between two rooms.

'Jamie spoke to the doctor on rounds today about the air pockets. It's something called subcutaneous emphysema.'

'From the PICC line?'

'Exactly.' Small grin.

We discuss the options: They can make small incisions to release the air or they can insert a chest tube to remove it. Both involve risk of infection and further discomfort.

We shake our heads at the same time.

'Okay, good,' Sam says. 'That was my feeling, too.'

He goes down the hallway to the bathroom and I go back to the room. The DA is gone. Yash is looking out the window. I sit in my chair and take his hand. He turns to me.

'Let's not argue, babe,' he says.

'No, let's not.' I sound like a Hemingway character.

'I was thinking about how Silas got you to forgive him with a postcard. He must be some writer.'

He's not done arguing.

'All those years I tried to reach you,' he says. 'And you shut me out. For one lapse of judgement.'

'It wasn't a lapse.'

'I was a lapse. I didn't mean it to be the end. I thought we could talk it over.'

'After you didn't show up? Why not before I left Paris?'

'I called on Christmas, remember? I wanted to talk then but you were in a rotten mood.'

'Things were hard that fall.'

'Hink, if I were given a hundred chances to do it over again, I would do it differently every single time. I loved you. I did. I just panicked a little.'

'I know, it was a real commitment.'

He shakes his head and lowers his mask. 'No, it wasn't that. Or not only that. I mean, I was committed to you.' His voice is much clearer, but the words come out slowly. 'I was at the beginning of my life. I wanted to do so much. And I was barely responsible for myself.' He stops to suck in more oxygen from the mask. 'I didn't know if I could carry us both, you know? Please don't look at me like that. I was broke. You were broke. And you had debt. We weren't being practical. I didn't want to be like my father, saddled with responsibility so young. History repeating itself. And I wasn't sure you understood the consequences—'

'Consequences? Let's talk about consequences, Yash. I was pregnant. I was five months pregnant in that Delta terminal waiting for you.'

And this is why I'd never told him. This slow shattering of his face. I never wanted to see it. He pulls away from me.

'Whar mer,' he says and is frustrated I can't understand him.

His oxygen has plummeted. I lift the mask back over his mouth and nose. 'Breathe,' I say. 'You have to breathe, babe.'

Above the mask his eyes are flashing back and forth.

Sam comes back in and around the bed to his spot on the other side.

Go away, I want to tell him. Leave us alone.

Yash makes a few sounds we can't understand.

He turns to Sam. 'Tell Cole not to come,' he says slowly and with great effort. 'I'm not going to make it to Tuesday.'

Sam and I look at each other. Yash shuts his eyes on us. Jamie comes in to check his vitals.

I leave the room before Sam can question me. I return to the alcove and sit with my back to everything. I take my phone out of my bag to check the time. The home screen is plastered with texts and missed calls from Silas, Jack, Harry, and the family group chat. My heart begins to race.

Jack has gotten a date for the brain stem surgery.

I scroll reluctantly through all the messages. Wednesday. This coming Wednesday. They want us in Houston by tomorrow night to begin pre-op testing on Monday morning. Jack's texts are ecstatic, all caps, with happy dancing emojis. The percentages, the numbers, mean nothing to him. All I can think about are the cold numbers and the risks—cognitive damage, paralysis, death—and all he can see is his life returned to him.

Silas' follow-up texts are logistical. He's gotten the three of us on a flight out of Portland tomorrow afternoon and a room with two queens at the hotel attached to the hospital, and has arranged for his favorite sub to take over all his classes for the week and for Harry to stay with his best friend Eli's family. Then Harry has written to say he has nothing going on in school the next few days and he wants to come with us and use his savings to pay for it. Silas writes that he has got Harry on our flight, too. Jack writes with more emojis that Harry is coming too. Harry has coped with Jack's illness by pretending it isn't happening. The first two surgeries were close by, in Boston, but he wouldn't come to the hospital. Now he's coming to Houston. The tears start as I write them back. I want to call Silas and talk to all of them, but I'm crying too hard and it would scare them.

'Jordan.' Sam sits in the little chair next mine. 'Are you okay?'

I hold up the phone. 'My son got a date for a big surgery.'

'That's good.' Yash has told him about Jack. 'When?'

'Wednesday. In Houston.' I wipe my face with the heels of my palms. 'Sorry. I can't seem to stop.' It feels a lot like being in Ray Hart's classroom, every awful terrifying thing flooding my system at once. 'Did Yash tell you?'

'No. He's not speaking to anyone. What happened?'

'I'm not sure he's going to talk to me again. I hope he'll talk to you.'

He nods. He reminds me of Silas then, the way he doesn't ask more. 'I'm going to get us some soup.'

He comes back in fifteen minutes with tomato soup, a grilled cheese sandwich, and a cup of tea. I've mostly stopped crying.

The food tastes good. He's gotten himself a grilled cheese, too.

'I really dreaded seeing you, Sam.'

He nods. 'I had some apprehension, too. Jordan, this is way too late, but I'm sorry. I truly am. I behaved badly.'

'I'm sorry, too. I wasn't very honest with you. Or anyone, really.'

'I knew. I probably knew before either of you knew. I think some perverse part of me wanted to see how it all played out.'

Down the hall Yash's mother is asking where Sam is. He doesn't get up.

'I can still see you on the ground,' he says. 'At that party. I didn't mean to push you.'

'I know that.'

'I can still see the way you were looking at me. When I think of my boys going off to college and behaving like that . . .' He shakes his head and crushes the sandwich wrapper into a small ball.

'Are you still religious?'

'No. Yash never told you?'

'We didn't speak of you. I know nothing about your life.'

He nods, taking this in. 'After Ivan died I had a crisis of faith. Existential. Explosive. It blew up my marriage, estranged me from my parents and siblings, my community. Yash was basically the only one left, he was right there for me. He carried me through it. He had his own grief about Ivan and his own struggles, and he carried me on his back for two years. I wanted to die and he wouldn't let me.' He leans closer to me. 'I don't know the whole story, but since the moment he met you, I know he would have done anything for you.'

'Except that one time when I really needed him to be there.'

'You probably won't believe me, but when he arrived at my door that night, I told him he was making a mistake. I knew how much he loved you. Because he'd risked our friendship for you. But he's complicated. I can't say I fully understand him even now. He chose to spend his life alone. It's not something that just happened to him.'

Yash's mom is calling our names. She finds us in the alcove. 'It's rounds,' she says sharply. A little glimmer of the anger Yash described.

Sam stands. I don't.

'You're not coming?'

'I think it's better if I don't.'

'All right. Don't leave, okay? When's your flight?'

'At nine.'

He looks at his watch. 'Stay till seven thirty. Whatever exchange you had with him, don't go early. Give him some time and have one more talk with him. Say goodbye. Goodbyes are important.'

He walks back down to Yash's room. I think that's the longest conversation Sam and I have ever had.

\* \* \*

Yash's mother perches on the edge of the chair Sam was sitting in. She's so small and brittle now. Pain turns women into birds, I think. I don't want to turn into a bird in a hospital hallway.

'Jared has gotten Venezuelan for dinner.'

'I just ate a sandwich.'

'I can't eat either. Can't eat a thing.'

She keeps such a distance from Yash. Or he keeps her at a distance. Whenever she comes into his room, I offer her my chair but she rarely takes it. The few times she did, they hardly spoke. She took his hand one time and he extracted it quickly. She prefers the doorway, the hallway, flanked by her sisters and Paige. We are not the same species, Yash said once. I am a human being and she is a two-ton albatross. She wants things from me I cannot give, he said another time, hanging up from a phone call with her. Sam fills her in on what the doctors say. I'm not sure she absorbs everything he says. I know the feeling well, that fog of fear as you strain to listen to the doctor.

Aunt Mo delivers her a plate piled with arepas, rice, black beans, and plantains. Uncle Percy comes out of the family room with two plates, one for Aunt Mo. EJ comes next. They eat leaning against the wall facing us.

Yash's mother pushes the fork through her rice but does not lift it to her mouth.

Brent and Bean come down the hallway.

'We're not playing sardines,' Aunt Mo says, reluctantly moving over for them to fit in the alcove. 'Peggy Lynn?'

Yash's mother nods.

'Do you remember when Alvin died, right here in this hospital?'

She grunts softly.

'Do you remember a few days before, they brought in a tray of snacks, an enormous tray, full of cookies and the like? Where is that tray? We need a tray like that for all these people.'

Yash's mother gets up and leaves without answering her and Aunt Mo turns her attention to me. 'He waited too long, didn't he? For someone so smart he could be awfully dumb, couldn't he?'

'I set him up with a girl once,' Bean says. 'Never again. She called me up the next day and said, "Who the fuck is Jordan?"'

EJ pushes himself off the wall and looms over me in my alcove. 'What *happened* between you two? I can't imagine any reason why you'd dump that guy. Heart of gold. Loyal as fuck.'

Aunt Mo takes the empty seat. 'Yashie wasn't easy to interpret, was he?' She lowers her voice. 'I think all that time he spent with Percy messed with him.'

'His father suspected he was CIA,' Paige says. 'Do you think he was CIA?'

'He gives me a book of yours every Christmas,' Aunt Bev says behind me. 'Every year. You've written so *many*.'

'Only four.'

'More than that. I get one every year.'

'The book business? Talk about a dying market,' Brent says. 'I hope to God you're transitioning to screen work. Now, streaming—that's what we call shit-ton profit potential. Did you see *Blood Force*? No book better than that series. You're hobbled by the lack of *visuals*. There's no competition with a screen. Sorry, but no matter how hard you try your dick is always going to be limp. I've read a book or two of yours. Started them, anyway. You're good at dialogue. You gotta go *after* it. Thank God Yash never tried to write books. You know that's what he wanted to do, right? He wouldn't have been happy doing that. It would have made him more of a recluse than he already was.'

I excuse myself and go back to Yash.

Arlo is alone with him, in a chair at the foot of his bed. He's playing the guitar. He's singing a song I know from a tape Yash made me when I was in grad school and we started talking again after Ivan died. It was a tape of gorgeous, depressing songs and I had it for years. Silas and I used to listen to it in his car when we were dating. This one was the best song on it. We always fast-forwarded to get to it.

I sit in my chair. Yash's mask is on tight and his eyes are closed. I take his hand and he doesn't respond.

'They loaded him up with meds,' Arlo says over his fingerpicking. 'He was getting twitchy.'

I squeeze his hand hard. I want him to wake up. But he's in a deep chemical sleep.

It's 7:43.

'Where's Sam?'

'On the phone with his kids.'

I kiss Yash's hand and let it go. I get my suitcase, say goodnight to Arlo, and walk out.

At the Hyatt, they give me a room that is the mirror opposite of the one from the night before. I collapse on the bed. My phone swarms with fresh texts. Where is the orange sleeping bag, Harry wants to know, he and Eli are going to sleep in a tent tonight. Jack hijacked Silas' phone and, in response to an earlier text to Silas asking about how Jack's day went, he wrote: *Jack is fine. If Jack had his own phone you could ask him directly and get many more details.*

The phone vibrates. It's Harry.

'It's not in the closet or the garage,' he says.

'Did you try the way-back of the car?'

'The car?'

'I keep it there in the winter. In case of a sudden blizzard on the highway.'

'You are so weird. Passing you to Dad.'

'Only one in the car?' Silas says. 'What about the rest of us?'

'If you guys were with me we'd be okay. We'd make a plan. Alone I would just need to get into a sleeping bag right away.'

'You at the airport?' Silas says. I barely pause and he says, 'You're not at the airport.'

'I'm going to have to meet you in Houston.'

'I bought you a flight from here with us.'

'I know. I have to change it.'

'I have been scrambling to put all the pieces together. I finally got Lorraine to take the dogs.'

'I'm sorry.'

'Planes aren't easy.' He means with Jack.

'I know.'

'The pressure.'

'I told him.'

'Told him what?' He's still on Jack.

'I told Yash.'

'Good for you.' This is mean, this sarcasm, coming from Silas.

'We had this fight right in the room with all these people around. And I told him and he wouldn't speak to me and I have to go back. I can't leave it like that.'

He is silent.

'I will meet you in Houston tomorrow. I promise I'll be there.'
'Is this about Yash? Or is it about Jack?'
'What do you mean?'
'You are his rock. He's never seen you scared. He looks at you and he thinks, I'm going to be okay.' He takes a breath. 'You cannot fall apart on him now.'
'I found it!' Harry says. He's grabbed the phone back. 'I love you, mother.' He hangs up.
Silas doesn't call me back.

# Sunday

A strip of blue light shines through the crack of room 508. I nudge the door open. They are both asleep, Sam curled on his side on the cot, two fists beneath his chin, a sharp pale ankle thrust out beyond the mattress, and Yash with his head tipped to one side the way he used to fall asleep reading, the johnny slipping off both shoulders, wires taped to his bare chest.

Oh, my love. My old love.

His breaths are faster, shallower. He's working so hard to breathe.

I drop into my chair and take his hand over the bedrail.

He makes a little whelp when he opens his eyes and sees me. 'I was scared you'd left,' he says, muffled through the mask.

I shake my head. 'I couldn't do that.'

His breathing, so short, so labored, disturbs us both.

Sam is snoring softly.

'Jack?' he says.

Sam must have told him.

'Wednesday.'

'You have to go home.'

'I'll meet them there tonight.'

'You should be with them now.'

'I want to be here a little while longer.'

'Then tell me,' Yash says. 'Please.'

I nod. 'First, let me just—' I examine the bedrail between us. I find the little button and push it. It slides down easily. He reaches for both my hands. We are much closer now.

'Tell me everything.'

I tell him. I tell him that I didn't know until early October, that I tried to write but ripped up every letter I started, that I called him at his dad's and at work and he never called me back. That I was five weeks, then six weeks, then seven. The French cut-off was ten. I didn't want to do anything without talking to him, I tell him, but I was scared to talk to him. I knew this was what had happened to his parents. He'd said once that if the laws had been different, he wouldn't have been born. I didn't know how he'd feel. I loved him so much, I tell him, I couldn't think straight. I couldn't think only for myself. 'It felt like a decision we had to make together but I couldn't reach you. By the time we talked in December there didn't seem any point. We'd be in New York in a week. I thought we'd figure it out in person.'

His head rocks back and forth. His breaths are too small.

'Yash.'

'Go on. Please go on.'

After Carson's, I tell him, I went to my mother's in Phoenix. By then I was clear about what I wanted to do. I tell him how my mom took care of me, how that healed something between us. I tell him about the agency and the photo of my first-choice couple. 'They reminded me of an older version of us. They looked like they really loved each other, amused each other.'

'You had the baby?'

'I did.'

He squeezes my fingers hard. He's still got a lot of strength.

'A girl,' I say.

Above the mask his forehead crumples. 'A daughter?'

'Yes.'

He can't say anything more for a while.

'Where is she?'

I shake my head. 'I don't know. They couldn't tell me. But every time I think of that photo, I know she's fine. They were good people. I know it.'

'Her name?'

'I don't know what they chose. I call her Daisy.'

He nods and tears run along the seam of his mask.

It's nice without the railing. We are very close, my face only a few inches from his. I drop my head on his shoulder. 'I had an hour with her. They let me give her a bottle. I wasn't allowed to nurse her. They said it would make it harder on us both. She took that bottle like she knew exactly what she was doing. My boys weren't like that. They sort of flopped around for a while before they figured it out.' I feel him let out a puff of air, a laugh or a small sob. 'Then a nurse came and got her. I checked a box, giving the agency permission to release my information to her. Whenever I move, I call and give them my new address. In case she asks for it.'

'She hasn't?'

'Not yet.'

'She's twenty-seven.'

I nod.

'When she does, will you tell her about me? Will you tell her I love her?'

'I will. Of course I will.'

'Tell her . . .' he says. I can't make out the rest. He's crying hard. He tries again. 'Tell her I'm always rooting for her.'

Neither of us can talk for a while. Our tears pool at his collarbone.

The only sound is Sam, snoring like a foghorn.

'You did all that alone.'

'I wasn't alone.'

'Without me.'

I look at the monitor. 87. Even with the mask. They will have to increase the liter flow.

'Do you think—' he stops for breath.

'Don't talk, Hink. Save your breath.'

'For what?'

I don't answer.

'Do you think I should have married?' He searches my face. 'Would I have been happier?'

'I don't know.'

'I don't think I would have been good at it. Maybe a quarter of the time. The rest of the time I'd want to be alone.'

I can see how true that is. How unhappy it would have made me.

'I have always loved you, though,' he says. 'Always always.'

The nurse Kelly comes in then. She smiles at Sam's snoring as she goes around his cot. I lift up my head and let go of Yash's left hand so she can pull a tube out of his IV and replace it with another.

When she leaves I put my head back on his shoulder.

'Do you think I'll be able to see her? Watch over her?'

'I think so,' I say. 'In some way.'

'Do you think it will be better?'

'Better than life?'

He nods.

'Yes,' I say, as if it's possible to imagine anything outside life.

'We have a child,' he says.

'I'm sorry.'
'For what?'
'Not telling you.'
I feel him shake his head. 'You told me. I'm so glad to know.'
We are quiet for a while.
I think he's fallen asleep, then he says, 'What do you make of death?'
'Death?' I stall.
'Do you have a personal theory?'
'You're going to think it's very Pollyanna.'
'No doubt.'
'You've spent your whole life reading everything. You should be telling me.'
'Say it.'
'Well, I believe we're all one. Same consciousness or awareness or whatever you want to call it. The universe is expanding now but soon—in a few more billion years—we'll start shrinking back again to what we were before the Big Bang. We'll get smaller and smaller and then for a moment we'll be a tiny speck. After that they say we'll be nothing—we won't exist at all inside a black hole. Then there'll be another bang and we'll return.'
'Surprise!' he says faintly.
'I think we desire unity because we have felt it before and we want to feel it again. It's our natural state.'
'Eternity as a concept is a bit terrifying,' he says.

'Only if time exists as we experience it. Which we know it does not. Without time, eternity loses its bite.'

'This is true.'

I wait for him to push against my theories. Instead he says, 'I don't know if I'm going to like billions of years of one consciousness.'

'You might get used to it.'

'I might. And I have a daughter.' His voice breaks and he squeezes my hands hard. 'It makes it easier somehow, Hink.'

We cry a little more and I feel his hands slowly go slack. He gives into sleep.

Sam rolls onto his side. Both feet are sticking out beyond the mattress now.

His open eyes make me jump.

He grins. 'I slept in.'

'You did.'

'Was I snoring?'

'Some.'

'I'm sorry. I know it's bad. Was he awake?'

'For a little while.'

'He sounds worse.'

'He is.'

His clothes are on a chair in the corner and he can't get to them.

'I'll go get the coffee,' I tell him.

I go down to the basement and stand in line. It's only hospital personnel at this hour. They wait in pairs or larger groups. Their chatter is comforting, these people who do such important work.

I was on a panel a few years ago with a philosopher who'd written a book on time. She said there were two prevailing theories, eternalism and presentism. Eternalism is the belief that everything that is, has been, and will be exists right now and forever, all at once. Presentism is the belief that only what exists in the present exists at all. Nothing before and nothing after. No exceptions. As we were walking off stage I asked her which she believed, and she told me she could make a strong case for either, but recently she was leaning toward presentism.

I didn't understand why she would lean toward presentism, why she would choose only the present moment—no past, no future—when she could have everything all at once for eternity. But standing here in line, with all these good people working to help others get better, it feels okay to me to have this moment and nothing else. It feels vast, open, beautiful. Only this right here right now. I feel happy. I have told him.

The cot is gone. Sam is dressed and back in his spot. Yash's eyes are open but he and Sam aren't talking. I hand Sam a coffee and a bagel and put Yash's coffee on his tray. I know he won't drink it. He can't take his mask off for that long now.

Yash reaches for my hand. He says something I can't understand. He says it again but the sounds don't turn into words. He can tell I didn't get it, but he doesn't try again.

'He needs more oxygen,' I say.

'We're at sixty,' Sam says.

I look at him. Sixty liters per minute. It doesn't go any higher than that.

A nurse we don't know comes in. She turns on the lights and lifts the shade. 'Why are all y'all in the pitch dark? Rise and shine. How are we this morning, my young man?'

Yash gives her a thumbs up.

Sam gets out of her way. She talks the whole time. She raises Yash up higher and she shifts the supports from one side to the other to prevent bed sores. Yash watches her and nods when she asks her questions and follows her with his eyes as she leaves the room.

'I didn't buy a couch,' he says clearly.

'Yes, you did,' Sam says. 'A red one.'

Yash shakes his head.

A few minutes later he makes this long awful sound deep in his throat, as if he were imitating a death rattle.

It surprises him as much as us. When he sees our faces, he chuckles. 'Still alive,' he says.

He makes a gesture to Sam and Sam lowers the bed a bit. Yash shuts his eyes. I see the boy I first knew. I see the boy sleeping on his back on the twin bed beneath the yellow bedspread.

An hour and a half later the family arrives. Yash has not woken up. His breaths are still very shallow, but they are not coming as fast. I watch them absorb the situation, the women first, the men more slowly. Sam takes Yash's mom out into the hallway.

A while later a doctor appears in the doorway. She speaks to Sam and me out in the hall. She says she suspects Yash will go unconscious soon, if he has not already, and that it could be another day or two or more. She is holding his DNR. Sam follows along better than I do. I nod and try to stay standing.

We go back into the room and Sam explains everything to Yash's mom and aunts.

Jamie comes in sometime after that and removes all the lines except the Foley catheter. She takes away the oxygen mask and the cannula and gently wipes his face with a cloth.

'His beautiful face,' Yash's mom says.

It is beautiful. It's so beautiful. Have I ever told him that?

He has deep red marks on his cheeks from the mask.

I brace myself for a terrible change without the mask, but his breathing is the same.

An orderly comes in with a platter of snacks, popcorn and cookies and chips in individually wrapped packages.

'The tray,' Aunt Mo says.

I come back from the bathroom and take my seat. The room is nearly empty, just Uncle Percy on his phone. I reach for Yash's hand. But this time it is not his hand in mine. It is my mother's hand. There is no other way to say this. It is my mother's hand. I can see that the hand I'm holding is Yash's, but what I feel are my mother's plump fingers, my mother's small, padded palm, the exact way her hand felt in mine when I was a little girl. It feels amazing.

Sam comes in with a woman named Jane from Yash's office and I have to let go of my mom and give Jane my seat. I eat a packet of Lorna Doones from the tray in a chair near Uncle Percy. Nothing truly mystical has happened to me in my life before this. But for a minute or two in this room, some sort of channel opened up, and my mom was able to squeeze her hand through to me.

Jane from his office pats Yash's arm and wipes her face many times. She says something very quietly to him then gets up and leaves. I return to my chair. My mother is gone. The hand is fully Yash's again. He doesn't turn when I touch it. He doesn't tell me about Jane. I will never know her story.

My phone says 6:10. I have to go. I have to go to Houston. I hug the aunts and uncles. Paige and Peggy Lynn. Jared bends his thin frame like a willow against me. His bushy hair catches briefly on my earring. I wish him luck.

I go over to Sam's side and we hug in silence for a long time.

I go back around and bend over you, my love. I brush my palm over your rooster's comb. 'I have loved you all my life,' I whisper. 'See you after the next bang.'

I spin my suitcase out of the corner. I look back once. Sam is holding both your hands.

I walk slowly to the elevator, like I have become a patient myself, like Hans Castorp falling sick at the sanatorium.

I push the green button and wait until a silver door slides open.

I thought it would feel better away from the hospital and at the airport, but it feels much worse. It's loud and crowded and no one else here knows Yash is dying.

I punch keys at the kiosk, get my boarding pass, and move unsteadily to security. I take off my shoes, lift my arms over my head in the body-scanner. I try to regroup in the bathroom. It takes me a long time to fit my suitcase in the stall with me. It's nighttime and I don't remember eating today. I don't look in the mirror while I wash my hands.

The central walkway is busy. I've already misplaced my boarding pass. I don't know the gate. I need to find a departures screen. I won't ever see you again. Where will you go? What will you be? I think of Aeneas going to look for his dead father in the Elysian Fields and how when he finds him he weeps as he tries to touch him, to hold him. Three times he tries and fails. His father is nothing more than a light wind in his arms.

I veer over to the windows facing the planes and runways lit up in the dark and sit on a bench. I think of our little red suit. I think of the tiny bed in Paris. La petite mort, you told me the Romantics called orgasm. The little death, we used to joke when you pulled out and your penis was like a small boneless animal, sweet and defenseless. Now you are facing the big death. Will you know I am remembering your penis? Will you watch over Daisy?

    I stand in line at Chipotle. I'm halfway through my burrito when I realize I haven't looked at a departures screen. I can see one across the food court. I leave my meal and go over to it. My flight leaves in forty-five minutes. A92. I head back to my burrito on the table and it looks like a half-eaten body on a tinfoil gurney. I leave it there and walk slowly away. I follow signs to my gate. People are moving so quickly in both directions. I can feel them look at me and look away fast. I can feel the blankness of my face. I don't want to bring death to Houston.

I have a middle seat toward the back of the plane. A young woman is reading a novel beside the window. In the aisle seat a man with enormous shoulders is on his phone, hurriedly trying to connect what look like tomatoes before they explode. Neither has left me an armrest. When the plane begins to back away from the gate, I have a bad feeling. Death feels close. I have brought death onto the plane. I find Jack's rock in my pocket and hold it tight. I used to have a superstition that the plane would go down unless I spoke to someone in my row before takeoff. I got out of this habit long ago, but tonight it feels like a safety measure I need to take.

'Headed home?' I ask the woman reading.

She looks up slowly, annoyed. 'Vacation.'

'Where to?' As a reader, I feel for her. I wish I could stop myself. If only she understood it is for the protection of everyone on this plane.

'Mexico City.'

'Oh, cool.'

She returns to her book—I can't see what it is from this angle—with a definitive twist away from me.

Liftoff has a soporific effect. I have to fight it. I don't want to sleep here in the middle seat. My head has a tendency to plummet forward without warning. But I am so tired. My body gets even heavier as the plane pushes itself up further from the earth. I feel drugged and desperate for escape. I want to forget everything and go unconscious. But I don't want to dream. I remember feeling this way when my mother died. I was afraid of dreaming about her, afraid of seeing her alive and having to lose her all over again. And I didn't dream of her, not for a long time. I can't stop my eyes from closing. When we level off and I can recline my seat so my head won't drop down, I slip into a longer, dreamless sleep.

## HEART THE LOVER

The captain's voice wakes me up when he tells the flight attendants to prepare for landing.

I wait in line on the jet bridge to get my suitcase. Warm, humid air comes through the open door down to the tarmac. Once I have my bag, I follow a man with yellow sneakers into the terminal, where the AC has eradicated the warm air. I follow signs to ground transportation. I hate airports. I hate hospitals.

I come to double glass doors with signs on them that say NO ENTRY BEYOND THIS POINT. I go through. My phone vibrates. It's a text from Sam.

Yash died.

I keep walking. Up ahead is an escalator. It seems to be moving much faster than regular escalators. My suitcase and I stand at the top. One metal step then another and another shoot out of the plate below my feet. Each one separates so fast from the one behind it and drops down. I can't seem to take a step before it's gone. It's too much with my suitcase, impossible that we will both make it safely onto one of these small corrugated islands of metal. I know it is strange, given the travel we have done together, this suitcase and I, the many escalators we have gone down. The silver steps continue to appear and separate and go down without us. I cannot move. I cannot do it. I cannot do any of it.

I step aside and watch people walk on and go down, some with bags much larger and heavier than mine. I have to get to the hotel. I have to get to my family. It is nearly midnight. I try again. I step. We make it, my suitcase and I. We are okay. I hold onto the black rubber handrail. We go down. I look for another ground transportation sign and I see Silas.

Silas is at the bottom of the escalator. I don't know how he is here. I didn't tell him the airline or the time. Did he get the boys to the hotel and come back for me? I don't know, but he is here and I step off and fall against him. He has to pull us out of the way of the people coming down behind me. He is in his big winter coat and I am in his arms and everything packed down inside me starts to rise. It comes up hard, in great heaves and groans then long quiet clicking sobs. He holds me so tight and we are there by the escalator a long time.

He holds me in the back of the taxi and in the hotel elevator. He pulls the key card out of his pocket and the door opens and we slip through quietly. The room is pitch-dark. I can sense my boys immediately, their sleep smells and breaths. Silas takes my hand and leads me in. I can make out two shapes now in the bed by the window. They are on their sides facing each other, mouths open, as if they fell asleep mid-sentence. I wrap my arms around Silas and we stand there beside the bed and my chest hurts with my love for the three of them.

I bend down and stroke Jack's thick hair. They will shave his head again and we'll see all the scars. Then they'll cut into his skull once more. This precious boy, half his childhood carved into the skin of his crown.

He will be okay. I don't know where this thought comes from, from me or from Silas, from Yash or my mother. It just comes to me. And it feels like an actual possibility.

Silas and I get into the other bed. I lie as close to him as I can, along the whole length of him. I cry some more and he holds me and I don't know where Yash is or what will happen when the sun comes up and the week begins. Maybe it's true what the philosopher said, that the past and the future don't exist, that this is the only moment we ever have, this moment right now and this moment and this—

'Casey,' Silas says in my ear, half asleep, pulling me closer, reading my mind. 'You're here.'